# A GENTLEMAN'S PROMISE

*Scandalous London Series*

## TAMARA GILL

A Gentleman's Promise
Scandalous London Series
Novella One

Copyright 2013 by Tamara Gill
Editing by Serena Tatti
Cover Art by EDH Graphics

This book is a work of fiction. The names, characters, places, and incidents are products of the writer's imagination or have been used fictitiously and are not to be construed as real. Any resemblance to persons, living or dead, actual events, locales or organizations is entirely coincidental.

All rights reserved. Without limiting the rights under copyright reserved above, no part of this publication may be reproduced, stored in or introduced into a database and retrieval system or transmitted in any form or any means (electronic, mechanical, photocopying, recording or otherwise) without the prior written permission of both the owner of copyright and the above publishers.

ISBN-13: 9781973267423

## KEEP IN CONTACT WITH TAMARA

Tamara loves hearing from readers and writers alike.
You can contact her through her website
www.tamaragill.com
or email her at tamaragillauthor@gmail.com.

## DEDICATION

*For my mother-in-law, Beverly.
Thanks for everything you do.*

CHAPTER 1

*Somerset England, 1818*

Charlotte waded out into the lake that ran behind her father's Somerset estate and swam toward the middle of the pond. The chilled water cooled her skin and was a welcome reprieve from the scorching summer heat, which England was experiencing that year.

Heat bore down on her head from the sun and she shrugged off the thought that she would freckle. It mattered little what she looked like anymore. Her future was as set as the seasons. The water was a refreshing change after a morning stuck in the stifling hot drawing room with Mama, going over invitations for the forthcoming season in London. Not that Charlotte cared who called or invited them to their events. Her father's decision was made and the marriage contracts were signed.

Charlotte floated onto her back and looked up at the endless blue sky above her. Not a cloud marred the horizon to hint a break in the endless heat wave. Not that she minded, for as long as this hot weather held, the longer her mama would demand that they stay in Somerset. And the longer she could remain unmarried.

The sound of a branch breaking underfoot pulled her from her musings and Charlotte treaded water while trying to find the source of the noise. *Please let it not be Gus.* Her eleven-year-old cousin was the most annoying, vexing boy. Forever reminding Charlotte that he was her father's heir and the future master of her home once the estate passed into his hands, following the demise of her father.

The little rascal seemed to forget she would be long married by then and that he wasn't inheriting a title, merely land, and a home. Little tyrant. Heir or not, she sometimes had the urge to bend him over her knee and spank him until he howled.

"Apologies, Miss King. I did not realize that you were swimming. Forgive my intrusion."

Charlotte shut her mouth with a snap at the sight of Lord Helsing's naked abdomen. His skin glistened and sweat beaded down the middle of his chest, just waiting for the cool spring water to wash it away.

Still unable to speak, her attention wavered to his lordship's skin-tight breeches, which were very snug indeed...Charlotte turned away and splashed some water on her face, hoped that the heat she felt beneath her skin was solely from the sun and not from seeing the man standing behind her on the bank.

"No apology required, my lord. Being as hot as it is today, I had thought to come for a cooling dip." She paused and wondered what he thought of her staring at him. Hoped against hope he did not realize what a profound reaction she always had when she was around him. Her stomach twisted into knots and her mouth dried, usually resulting in her inability to form words. Blushing was the least of her problems.

"Well, I will take your leave. Good day, Miss King."

Charlotte turned about, savoring the vision of his back, which was indeed as pleasing as his front. "I was just about to leave. You may stay and swim if you wish."

His dark, hooded gaze fixed on her and Charlotte fought not to die of embarrassment. They had been friends once. Had in fact been neighbors since they were children. But school and social circles soon placed a wedge between their friendship. As was the case for many children in such circumstances.

"If you're sure, Miss King? I wouldn't wish to impose upon you."

"If my lord would be kind enough to turn for a moment to afford me some privacy, I could emerge from the water," she said, swimming toward the shore.

Lord Helsing turned around and waited for her. Charlotte wrung out her soaked shift as best she could before pulling on her summer gown that buttoned up at the front. Her dress clung to her and was uncomfortable against her skin but she ignored it. The fact that Lord Helsing, one of the most popular gentlemen in town was making conversation with her was too good an opportunity to believe.

"I'm ready, my lord."

Lord Helsing looked over his shoulder and met her gaze. He smiled and turned before making his way to the bank of the lake and sitting started to take off his boots. Charlotte watched as he slid his stockings off, his long feet oddly different to hers. She'd never seen a man's feet before.

"Do you mind if I take a swim, Miss King?" he asked, his brows raised.

Charlotte shook her head and then cleared her throat. "No, of course not."

Charlotte bit her lip as she watched his lordship dive under the water before emerging with a sigh of pleasure. A well-muscled arm came out of the water and pushed back a lock of hair that had fallen over his brow and the breath in her lungs seized. Never had she been so close to a man only half dressed, not to mention a man who unsettled her with just a glance.

"Delightful," he said.

She couldn't have worded her thoughts better.

"I thought you would be in town, Miss King. Is this not your debut year?"

Charlotte hid her stockings in her pocket and looked about for her shoes. "We're due up any day. As soon as this dratted heat abates, Mother will take me to London." She frowned. "I'm engaged to be married, my lord. Did you know?"

He swam toward the bank, the shock of her statement easy to read on his features.

"I had not heard. Congratulations." He paused. "May I ask who the lucky fellow is?"

"Viscount Remmick, my lord." Charlotte watched to see if Lord Helsing showed some sort of reaction to her words. Or more truthfully, hoped he would. Yet, his easy smile at her words dashed any hopes she may have had that he may have found the news unacceptable. Hopes that he would, in fact, run from the water, pick her up and declare his undying love to her.

Instead, he swam back into the centre of the pond and dived out of sight. By the time he had resurfaced, Charlotte was ready to leave.

"It was a pleasure to see you again, my lord. It had been a long time. I hope we may meet again in town?"

"I may see you tomorrow as I have business with your father. But if not, perhaps our paths will cross in London as you say."

Charlotte discreetly drank in one last sight of him before she turned and walked away. Made sure that she didn't look back. Not once.

## CHAPTER 2

Mason handed his horse to the waiting groom and looked up at the red brick Tudor mansion which Charlotte called home. Granted the house was not as grand as his estate, Dellage, but it was beautiful, with the ivy vines and hollyhocks that grew wild on and around its base.

He breathed in deep the smells of a home he knew as well as his own and hoped the missive he'd sent around yesterday to call on Mr King had been received.

Mason met the welcoming gaze of the footman, who opened the door. "Lord Helsing to see Mr. King," he said. The cooling air of the foyer was a welcome reprieve from the heat outside.

The footman having not taken two steps, stopped when Mr King, a tall, stout man, stepped out of the library. When he was young, Charlotte's father used to scare him with his size and boisterousness, but not anymore. Now, the older gentleman seemed jolly instead of daunting. Welcoming instead of annoyed at his presence.

"Welcome, my lord. Please," Mr King said, gesturing him toward the library. "Join me."

Mason followed Mr King into the room. Books littered the walls, along with scrolls and papers placed on any available surface. Unable to see a chair under the assortment of paper work, Mason stood before the desk instead. Mr King laughed and picked up the papers from a chair, allowing him to sit.

"Thank you," Mason said, taking a seat.

"What brings you to our humble establishment, my lord? I hope everything is well at Dellage." Mr King sat behind his desk and steepled his fingers over his rotund stomach.

Mason cleared his throat. "Very well, thank you, no reason for concern on that score," he replied. "No, my business today involves your daughter, Miss King. It's come to my attention she's to marry Lord Remmick and I'm here as an old family friend and neighbor to urge you caution and perhaps persuade you to break the marriage contract."

Mr King sat shocked into silence, his face an awful pasty-white color that didn't bode well for the gentleman's health.

"Are you unwell?" Mason asked, becoming concerned when Charlotte's father reached out for his brandy, downing it in one gulp.

Mr King coughed. "Confused is all. How is it you care what Charlotte does and who she marries? You do understand she has been promised these past two months to Viscount Remmick. It's a little late for neighborly concern now."

Mason nodded. "I've been away on my estates and came home as soon as I'd heard the rumor. I had hoped your daughter would make a more suitable match, and with all due respect, Mr King, Lord Remmick is not." The thought of the lovely Charlotte married to a rogue and one whose past was as sketchy as his health sent shivers of revulsion down his spine.

"Lord Remmick met Charlotte in London before her debut and travelled down here and proposed only two months past. She accepted him, of course. How is it," Mr King said, rising from his chair to refill his brandy glass, "that an Earl, no matter how close a neighbor, would care what my daughter did with her life? We have not entertained in the same circles and I have not seen much of you since you left for Eton and then Cambridge. It does seem odd that you should take an interest now, my lord."

Mason took a moment to gather his wits. His mind whirred with the truth of Mr King's words. True, he hadn't had a lot to do with his neighbors in recent years, but that didn't change the fact that Charlotte had been his closest childhood friend. They were no longer as close as they had been due to the fact they'd grown up, moved in different circles and had vastly different friends, but that didn't mean he did not care for her.

"My lord?" Mr King prompted.

Mason took a calming breath and met the speculative eyes of Charlotte's father. "I suppose as children, when my parents were alive and we stayed at Dellage, a friendship formed between Miss King and myself. I care for her and do not wish to see her hurt in any way. My concern stems from my knowledge of Lord Remmick. He is unsuitable match for Charlotte."

"Charlotte, my lord? You mean, Miss King."

Mason refused to squirm under Mr King's inquisitive stare. "Of course, Miss King," he said.

Mr King sat back in his chair and sighed. "You are asking me if Charlotte can rescind her agreement due to the fact Lord Remmick does not meet your standard of husband for her."

"That is exactly what I'm asking. I'm sure you've heard the rumors about Lord Remmick. Now, I'm not the type of man to sully another's reputation, but when it comes to your daughter's choice in husband, I think it only right I let you know the rumors are true. To think of Miss King subjected to his way of life would be something I would not wish on such a gentle and sensitive young woman." Mason watched surprise then distaste flow over Mr. King's visage. He was aware that the way he was speaking was very insulting to Charlotte's betrothed and could be termed forward at best, yet Charlotte deserved better than a marriage filled with immoral behavior, mostly achieved around the streets and lanes of Covent Garden and the Cyprians who paraded their wares there.

"The contracts have been signed. There is nothing to be done. Charlotte will be Viscountess Remmick by the end of the season. I'm confident my daughter is happy with her choice." Mr. King rang a bell on his desk and stood. "I understand your concern, my lord. But I think as her father that I know what is best for her. She will be in safe and loving hands I assure you."

Mason remained seated, tried and failed at keeping his opinions to himself. "I apologize if you think I've spoken out of turn, but when the happiness of your daughter is at risk, I'm sure you wouldn't wish to ignore my concerns. Are you not the least worried by Lord Remmick's seedy lifestyle? He's a rogue. A man rumored to have caught an unspeakable infection. How could you give your permission, Mr. King?" Mason felt his temper getting away from him and he took a calming breath.

Mr. King waved the footman away who came in at the raised voices. He sighed. "It was her choice. I've always raised my children to be of independent thought. Lord Remmick asked for her hand and Charlotte said yes, it was simple as that." Mr King smiled, the action bordering disdain. "I am aware of his misdemeanors and he has promised to remedy his lifestyle. That is enough for me."

Mason snorted. "And you believed him." He paused and ran a hand through his hair. How could the fellow be so blind? "Does Charlotte know he's poor? He may be titled but all but his pockets are for rent." Mason caught a flicker of anger in Mr. King's eyes, although whether over his questioning or enlightening of Lord Remmick's situation he couldn't tell.

"She knows. Fortunately for Charlotte, her dowry will amply provide for them both and therefore there is no reason for concern. Now, if you'll excuse me, my lord, I have a luncheon with my family to attend."

Mason stood. "This is a mistake. You're letting your eldest daughter make the biggest blunder of her life. I hope, Mr King, that she doesn't live to regret her choice." He walked out of the room without another word. The man didn't seem to have any principles. It made Mason wonder if they'd really told Charlotte the truth of Lord Remmick's situation.

He opened the front door and started when the man himself stood at the threshold about to tap the knocker. "Lord Remmick," Mason said, stepping past him.

His lordship smiled and turned. "Lord Helsing, I was unaware that you were to join us for luncheon."

"I'm just leaving," Mason said, relieved to see his horse being led from the stable.

"Please, do not leave on my account." Lord Remmick laughed. "You know, given enough blunt I'm always willing to share." His lordship winked, before stepping inside.

Mason stood still in shock before anger thrummed hot

in his veins along with helplessness. Charlotte's marriage to that fiend was not what she deserved. He shook his head. Her father ought to be horsewhipped.

He cantered down the graveled, maple-lined drive and images of Charlotte, the sweet, young woman, as pure as a breath of spring air beneath the filthy, diseased rogue haunted him. He pushed his horse into a gallop. He should have courted her himself. At least then she would have the life she deserved. He chastised himself that he hadn't sought her out in London. But never had it occurred to him that she would accept the first marriage proposal she received. It was not uncommon for women to have two seasons before they made their choice. Mason sighed, knowing why she had done so. Charlotte had always been impatient, ready to do and experience everything she could. It would seem she included marriage on her list of many things to achieve early.

He could always bribe Lord Remmick to walk away. Maybe even talk Charlotte into breaking the contract. He was nearing thirty and it was time he thought of marrying. And he knew Charlotte better than any other woman. They would get along well enough.

But Remmick was selfish. It would only be a matter of time before he was back and demanding more funds, until nothing was left of his or Charlotte's fortune. Helsing swore and spurred his horse on.

He would have to let her go and hope for the best. To avoid any uncomfortable meetings, he would close up Dellage and leave for London. Travel in the cool of the evening to limit the strain on his horse. He would not return to Somerset until after Miss King was married and settled.

Happily so, with any luck.

## CHAPTER 3

"Was that Lord Helsing I just saw, leaving in a cloud of dust?" Charlotte placed her gloves on her father's desk and poured herself a cup of lemonade. The cool, sour drink went some way towards bringing her body temperature down. Not wholly due to the extreme heat which summer was bestowing on them, but from the view of Mason's departing backside as he galloped down the drive on his horse.

"Yes, it was," her father replied. "I've just had the oddest conversation with the man. It seems he has concerns with whom you've agreed to marry."

"That is exactly what I wished to speak to you about." Charlotte came to stand before him. "I do not think Lord Remmick and myself are well suited. I received a letter today from Amelia, Lady Furrow and not to be impolite papa, she mentioned some terrible rumors going around London in relation to my betrothed. I don't wish to make a mistake."

Her father laughed. "You're just confused, my dear. Should I break the contract and grant you your wish, will you come to me in three months and say the same thing about some other gentleman who asks for your hand? The contracts are signed and to break a contract would be scandalous, not to mention, too expensive, even for me."

Charlotte started at her father's insight. Was she just experiencing wedding jitters, as some women had mentioned to her? Perhaps, yet sometimes, deep in Lord Remmick's eyes she noted an emotion that left her fearful and uneasy. Not to mention her friend's letter and the rumors, some of which made her blush.

Her father sighed. "You'll see, my dear" he said standing. "Lord Remmick is a vibrant, kind, sort of gentleman. He'll treat you well and keep you amused. Trust me," her father said, kissing her cheek just as the library door opened.

"Ah, Lord Remmick, so glad you could join us today."

Charlotte whirled around having been unaware that his lordship was to join them. He wasn't a man usually swayed to venture out of the city. And yet here he was. He strolled toward them like a man without a care. And Charlotte supposed that now her dowry was only a wedding ceremony away, he didn't have any.

Today he was dressed in a bottle green double-breasted coat and nankeen breeches, with shining black top-boots. Lord Remmick looked like a dandy who should be strolling the lawns of Hyde Park instead of her father's library. And although not an overly tall man, his roguish charm often turned heads at balls and parties. Even Charlotte had to admit that when she'd first met him, his quick wit, carefree laugh and perfect attire had bedazzled her. Perhaps she'd imagined that look in his eye that threw shivers of dread down her spine. For the gentleman before her was all charm and finesse.

"My lord Remmick. Welcome to our home." Charlotte curtsied. "I'm so glad you decided to join us."

His lordship flopped himself down on to a chair and started to pull off his gloves. "Well, how could I refuse an invitation to dine with my future family? London is not so very far away. I'll be back in the capital by tomorrow night as it is."

"So soon?" she asked. "Perhaps you could extend your stay with us for a day or two?" Which would enable her to study him more closely, away from the ton and all its diversions. His look of horror at her suggestion put paid to her idea.

"Alas, I cannot. Apologies, Mr. King, Charlotte. But I really must be in London by tomorrow."

"Well, that is a shame, my lord." Her father beckoned toward the door. "The lunch gong has sounded. Shall we?"

Lunch was uneventful. Lord Remmick spoke endlessly of London life and the balls Charlotte would soon be attending with him. Night after night stretched before her, an endless parade, it seemed, of entertainments that he expected her to enjoy along with him.

Nervousness caused butterflies to flutter in her stomach. Although not unaccustomed to the ton and their ways, Charlotte couldn't help feeling a little like a trophy, an ornament that had filled his pockets with coin. After a lengthy discussion on the improvements he would do to their London townhouse and his Surrey estate, Charlotte had heard enough for one day.

"If you'll forgive me, father. But I seem to have a headache. I think I'll lie down for a little while."

Her mother looked up from her syllabub dessert. "Are you alright, my dear? Would you like me to order a tisane for you?"

"That would be lovely. Thank you, mama." Charlotte stood and curtsied. "I will see you all a little later."

"I look forward to it."

Charlotte started at Lord Remmick's lowered tone and piercing gaze that seemed more like a wish to devour her later than to just see her.

She walked slowly upstairs and on reaching her room, received her tisane. While her maid helped her undress, her mind turned to Lord Helsing only a few short miles away. Was he right at this moment undressing that fine, masculine body and crawling into his silk sheets to sleep away the hot afternoon? Not that she knew what type of linen he had, but one could dream.

Charlotte dismissed her maid and locked the door, not trusting Lord Remmick to adhere to the rules of no touching before marriage. And marry his lordship she would. Brought up to believe and trust in her father, she felt he would not lie to her when stating that his lordship was worthy of her hand. That he would be a kind and loving husband.

And it was a little late to worry over her choice now. She'd always been prone to acting hastily. A terrible fault which her mother had forever been trying to banish from her eldest daughter, since she was a child.

What a shame Lord Helsing hadn't approached her the previous season. To come up to her and ask her to dance. To talk to her as they'd talked together as children. Her future could have been very different indeed, had he courted her instead. But he hadn't and now she was promised to another. It would be wrong of her to break the understanding. She would marry Lord Remmick at the beginning of the next season and she would wish Lord Helsing happiness with whomsoever he chose.

CHAPTER 4

*Two Years Later – Bath*

Mason screwed up the letter from his cousin Amelia, Lady Furrow, and swore. He threw the missive into the fire and sat at his desk to hasten a reply. Anger thrummed through his veins that he'd been correct two years before and that his fears had been realized.

Poor, Charlotte!

"Problem?" His friend George, Lord Mountbatten asked from the settee on which he lay, his cravat untied and his hair mussed from lack of sleep.

Mason sighed and blotted the missive closed. "Yes. I've had a letter from my cousin with some distressing news of an old neighbor of mine. I have to return to London."

George sat up. "When? You can't miss Lady Lancer's ball. Her ladyship will never forgive you."

"It's probably best I leave in any case. Her daughter has been making advances that I'm not reciprocating, if you get my meaning."

His friend laughed. "I understand perfectly well…unfortunately."

Mason stood and rang for a servant. He looked down at his friend and wondered how he could get him to leave without being rude. For weeks George had used his library as a sleeping quarter. Having arrived in Bath he had taken up residence with Mason for a short duration which had turned into a month's long stay. "Why don't you go up to one of the guest rooms," he said. "You're more than welcome to stay and not use my settee as your bed."

"I should return to my father's townhouse. I apologize for being a hindrance. But whenever I'm at home, mama is bothering me with the names of ladies she wishes me to meet. My head spins with the amount she says are worthy of me."

A footman entered and Mason gave him the missive and instructions on his departure early the following morning. He would be back in the capital in a day or so and would see for himself if what Amelia had written was true.

He smiled at the thought of Charlotte and wondered if she'd changed in the years since he'd seen her last. Having married Lord Remmick he hadn't let his mind wonder as to how she was. But now… Now he could not stay away.

Bath was beautiful, and although the society was limited, it afforded him time to make his choice. Unfortunately, he hadn't found the woman he'd wanted to marry here, but the season was young and travelling back to London would widen the possibilities. First, though, he had to ensure Charlotte wasn't as Amelia stated in her letters.

The thought she may be unhappy sent a chill down his spine. A woman of such beauty, inside and out, deserved only the best and he would ensure she was treated with such and nothing else.

"Who was it you said wrote to you from London?"

Pulled from his thoughts, Mason met the inquisitive gaze of his friend. "Lady Furrow, my cousin."

"You're up to something. I want to know what"

Mason sat on the settee across from George. "I'm not up to anything. Not yet at least. Ask me again when I see you in town."

"You have that look about you that I haven't seen since you were plotting the comeuppance of our old professor in Cambridge. Tell me."

"I will tell you nothing. Now go home before your mama comes looking for you. It wouldn't be the first time."

George groaned. "I'm leaving" he said sitting up and tidying his hair. "I have to pack my things."

"What for? Where are you off to now?" Mason asked.

"London. I can't have you having all the fun in town while I'm up here without anyone to keep me amused. Where's the fun in that?"

Mason laughed. "For what I have planned, 'fun' isn't a term I'd use."

"Better and better."

Mason watched as his closest friend waved and walked out the door. He stood and poured himself a brandy and watched as the flames licked at the wood. He would miss Bath and its quieter society. This home and the staff who kept the townhouse ready for him all year round. For the past two years the break from London and the ton was a welcome reprieve. But all good things must come to an end and unfortunately, his time here had as well.

London called as so too did his need to ensure that his childhood friend was safe, happy and being treated in the way all women should be treated. With respect.

CHAPTER 5

*London*

The crack across Charlotte's jaw knocked her over and left her splayed upon the Aubusson rug. For a moment, blackness was all she could see, before the reality of what her husband, James, had done brought her back to consciousness.

She sat up and took a calming breath. Would not, no matter how many times he assaulted her, let him see her cry.

"Are you happy? See what you made me do," he said coming over and pulling her to her feet. He sat her on the end of the bed and clasped her jaw in a punishing grip.

Charlotte swallowed her fear and helplessness. She'd married a monster, camouflaged behind a suit and top hat. She remained quiet as he inspected what his actions had done to her face.

"You're not fit to be seen in public now. You'll stay home and miss Lord and Lady Furrow's ball. I'll make your excuses." James stood and went to stand before her dressing table mirror. Charlotte watched him fix his cravat and run a hand through his hair. To anyone else, he looked handsome, regal and in control of his life. But he was not. He was the ugliest man she had ever known. A man who could not control the disease inside of him that made him cruel and rotten to the core.

"Amelia will ask questions if I'm not there. Perhaps you should have thought of that before you struck me."

He cast a dismissing glance and walked to the door. "She will not or I'll smack that bitch across the face as well. Or threaten to tell her husband of our affair."

Charlotte gasped. "You lie. Amelia would never betray Lord Furrow."

James grinned. "Of course she wouldn't, but he's a jealous and doting husband. Weak when it comes to his beautiful wife. It would not take much for me to plant the seed of disloyalty and for it to fester under his skin. No matter if it were true or false."

Charlotte watched him go, then walked over to her toilette and dampened a cloth to hold against her face. A dull ache ran through her jaw and a headache began to thump at her temples.

She caught her reflection in the mirror across the room and what she saw left her ashamed. How could her life have turned out so wrong? From the first night of her marriage to James, she'd noticed his personality change.

No longer was he attentive and loving, but indifferent and dismissive. He'd cancelled their wedding trip to the continent, stating he'd not felt up to such a lengthy journey. Instead they'd travelled to London where Charlotte was dropped off at their Grosvenor Square townhouse, while her husband took himself off elsewhere.

After that, endless nights of his drunkenness had

occurred. And when she'd chastised him over his behavior and conduct he'd hit her for the very first time.

Her life had continued down that same vein. Of course, Charlotte had learnt not to say anything anymore, for fear that one day he'd strike her so hard she wouldn't wake up.

Sometimes she wished she would not.

Tears streamed down her cheeks and she swiped them away, anger replacing helplessness and shame.

"My lady, do you wish me to help you undress for bed?"

Charlotte looked up and nodded for her maid to enter. The servants had long ago learnt to live with their quick-tempered master. Like Charlotte, they stayed away from his lordship and went about their jobs, making sure they were thorough with their duties lest his lordship was displeased.

"Can you have a tisane made up for me? And bring up a cup of tea before you retire for the night."

"Yes m'lady."

Stripping down to her chemise, Charlotte crawled into bed and wondered what she could do to change her circumstances. Divorce wasn't an option, but she supposed she could always just leave. But then James would win. Would in fact have everything she had brought to the marriage. All her money.

Charlotte thumped the quilt, frustration boiling in her blood. If only he would die. Then all her problems would be solved. But no matter what type of debauchery he lived in the bowels of London, he hadn't yet angered the wrong type of people. Probably because, she mused, he *was* the wrong type of people.

Charlotte thanked her maid as she placed the tisane and tea on the side table. There was nothing she could do besides try and make the best of a terrible situation and hope one day James would change. She drank down the tisane then picked up her tea, taking a sip to remove the unpleasant taste.

She sighed as the sweet brew soothed her a little. Tomorrow was a new day and in three days time she was to attend Lord and Lady Venning's soiree, an event she'd been looking forward to for quite some time.

Not because she was overly close with her ladyship but because Charlotte had found out about one particular guest who was to attend.

It was none other than her childhood friend Lord Helsing. Just the thought of seeing him after such a long time sent excitement through her veins. Would he speak to her or dismiss her? Not since their meeting at her family lake had she seen him. She could have written and kept in contact she supposed, yet whenever she tried, the fear that he would think of her as forward made her throw the letters away instead.

Charlotte finished her tea and sighed. If only she'd stood firm with her father and demanded to be released of the understanding with James, her life could have been be so different now. Not even the blessing of children to take the edge from the life she lived.

Blowing out the candle Charlotte lay down and tried to not feel sorry for herself. She had made her choice, and it had been wrong. It was as simple and unfortunate as that.

Lady Venning had outdone herself with her decorations for the soiree. Everywhere Charlotte looked, roses were gathered in bunches around the corners of the room and before the magnificent unlit fireplaces. The evening was warm and the scent was divine, much nicer than the smell of cigars and sweat from having too many people in a room all at once.

Charlotte looked down at her evening gown of dark blue crepe and adjusted her bodice a little. Her fingers shook and she mentally chastised herself for being nervous. Lord Helsing may not even make an appearance. And even if he did, there was no reason for him to seek her out.

After Lord Helsing had left their home that long ago summer's day, he'd changed too. Some would say for the better, if that were at all possible. He had returned to London that following season and thrown himself into the tonnish life with abandon, before taking himself off to Bath to enjoy the small society there.

No longer was he a man who watched life go by before him. Now Lord Helsing enjoyed the ton and all its entertainments. Women spoke of him with wistfulness and affection and Charlotte wasn't naive enough to believe that he ever spent his nights lonely.

Married women spoke of his bedroom exploits and accomplishments as if they were discussing the latest dress patterns in *La Belle Assemblée*. Heat travelled up her neck at the thought and she took a cooling sip of her wine.

Charlotte frowned, pondering on how she'd missed him these past two years. Lord Helsing, it seemed, was determined not to meet her in society, no matter what his words had been the last day they met. But he was in town and no one who was anyone turned down Lord and Lady Venning's invitation. Lord Helsing would be no different.

Charlotte smiled and watched as Amelia strode toward her.

"Charlotte darling, I'm so glad you're here. How are you, dearest?" she asked, giving her a pointed stare.

"I'm fine, truly. I'm sorry I missed your ball." She clasped her best friend's hand.

"You were missed. Your husband made his excuses for you, but I knew as soon as I realized you were not with him what he'd done. I wanted to come and check on you, but Charles wouldn't let me. Not," she said, meeting Charlotte's gaze, "that he wasn't concerned also, but because we were, after all, the hosts."

Charlotte swallowed the lump wedged in her throat over her friend's concern. "Thank you. But I'm better now. In fact, I haven't seen James since he left for your ball. I hope he doesn't arrive here tonight and make trouble."

"He wouldn't dare." Amelia frowned. "Charlotte you know Charles and I would be more than willing to have you stay with us. You need to leave your husband and soon. Before he kills you with his outbursts. This is no way to live your life."

Charlotte bit back her tears. She knew the truth of her situation and Amelia was right. One day James would hit her so hard that she'd never recover. It was only a matter of time. But should she leave, her family would be disgraced, her sisters' prospects shattered like a pane of glass. No, she couldn't leave her husband, even for her own sake.

"You're so kind. And I know how much you care. But I cannot. Please, let's not discuss this now. I'm simply enjoying the freedom of being at a soiree without James hovering over me like a cloak; please let me forget my cares for a little while."

Amelia kissed her cheek. "Of course, darling. Whatever you wish, I'm just concerned for your wellbeing, that's all."

Charlotte smiled. "I know you are. Now, tell me," she said, changing the subject. "How are you feeling? Are the mornings still the worst for you?"

"Yes," Amelia said, placing her hand discreetly on her

belly, as if to guard the little life that grew inside. "The mornings are terrible. Thank goodness I'm well enough in the evenings to attend the season's entertainments. I don't know how I'd survive otherwise."

Charlotte smiled while a pang of envy shot through her. Not once in the two years she'd been married had she bore a living child. It was another reason why James abhorred her. In his eyes, she was a barren, useless piece of common baggage that he should never have married.

When Charlotte had reminded him her common class had saved his estate and him against his debtors, she'd paid for it by being bedridden for a week. The belting he'd inflicted had been one of the worst she'd ever had. And she'd learnt to curb her tongue from that point onwards. As much as doing so irked her greatly.

"Charlotte are you well?"

She started out of her musings and smiled. "Of course, just lost in thought, that's all. What were you saying?"

"Only that Lord Helsing has arrived. And that he's looking directly at you."

Charlotte looked up and locked eyes with Mason immediately. It was almost as if an invisible line connected them across the sea of heads. She smiled and watched as he nodded in greeting before moving off to join another party his side of the room.

"He's as handsome as ever. Why did you never tell me you were neighbors as children? I had to find out about it by Lady Sisily."

Charlotte started at the question having never thought to tell Amelia of their childhood friendship. It was bad enough just to think about Mason and the silly passion she'd once held for him.

"I'm sorry, Amelia. I suppose it slipped my mind. It's been, after all, two years since I saw him last."

Amelia cast her a speculative look, then turned her attention back to the throng. "Well, I suppose you'll be able to catch up tonight. And without Lord Remmick here, I'm sure you'll be able to relax a little and enjoy your reunion."

Charlotte swallowed. It was silly really to be nervous about talking to Lord Helsing again. Granted, they hadn't been close for many years, but after that one day near the lake, everything had changed for Charlotte. He'd been kind and attentive like the old days, something that she longed for her husband to be now. Not that he ever would be.

She caught sight of his lordship strolling through the throng before he asked a young debutante with doe eyes to dance. A pang of jealousy shot through her and Charlotte chastised herself. She was married and he was not. Of course, he could dance with whomsoever he wished.

She watched as he waltzed about the room with the beautiful, young woman, his grace and ease obvious to any who observed. Lord Helsing seemed much broader across the shoulders and his hair was a little less tidy, and yet, to Charlotte, he was the handsomest man present.

"Perhaps it is best that you stop your inspection of Lord Helsing, dearest as your husband just stumbled through the door."

Charlotte watched in horror as James staggered into the room, needing the wall and a few guests for support. His cravat hung about his neck and his shirt gaped open at his throat. He looked sweaty and not at all well. People gasped and moved out of his way as James looked about the room.

For her.

Charlotte stepped away from Amelia and started to walk toward him, thankful the minstrels continued to play and people danced. He stood upright as she came to his side.

"I'm so pleased to see you, dear James." She smiled to hide her distaste. "Amelia and I are over the other side of the room. Come and sit with us there."

He gave her a dismissing look and pulled his arm from her hand. Charlotte let him go and followed as he swayed toward her friend. Embarrassment threatened to choke her. It felt as if everyone watched the spectacle that was their marriage. A prickling of heat suffused her cheeks and Charlotte lifted her chin, not willing to cower under the collective mocking and curious gazes.

James flopped into a chair and sprawled like a man who was about to go to sleep. Charlotte sat beside him, summoning a footman for some water.

"James, you need to sit up. You're at Lord Venning's home and you know how he detests drunkenness and rowdy behavior."

"Bite your tongue, woman. Who are you, a commoner, to tell a Viscount how to behave?"

Amelia sat beside James and smiled. "She has every right, as your Viscountess. Furthermore, your sickly pallor and untidy attire is hardly appropriate for polite society. You ought to be ashamed of yourself embarrassing your wife in such a way, Lord Remmick." Amelia stood. "I will seek you out later, my dear."

Charlotte nodded and waited for James's temper to take hold. Amelia had every right to hate him, why she hated him too now. There was no affection left in their marriage. James had extinguished that the first time he hit her.

"How dare that bitch speak to me so? I ought to—"

"Remember where you are, James." Charlotte handed him a drink. "Sit up and drink this and try and look the gentleman. You do know your cravat is untied?" Charlotte smiled at two passing matrons and tried not to imagine what they must be thinking.

James looked down at his shirt and laughed. "Well, I'll be. Seems I didn't tie it up after. Well, let me just say she had the longest legs, wrapped them nicely about my hips while I gave it to her up against a deserted lane's wall." He smirked and met Charlotte's gaze. "You don't mind do you, my lady. Since you no longer spread your legs for me, I have to find my enjoyment elsewhere."

Charlotte shuddered and looked about to ensure no one was within hearing range. "What you do in your spare time is no concern of mine, but you must, when appearing at social events, at least look like the Viscount you were born to be."

"She was a ripe beauty as well. New to London from up north somewhere. With just one touch I was able to make her as wet as the Thames between her legs. The sweetest woman I've tasted in an age. Would you like to kiss me and find out, my dear?"

"You're a vile, piece of human flesh and I'm ashamed to call you my husband."

James clasped her jaw and Charlotte stilled before he gathered his wits and sat back laughing. "You'll pay for that later."

Tears threatened and Charlotte bit the inside of her lip. Hard. Why wouldn't he just leave? Go back to the cesspit he was so fond of in the East end of town and let her be?

CHAPTER 6

Mason watched Charlotte and Lord Remmick argue from across the room and the blood in his veins ran cold when he saw his lordship clasp Charlotte's delicate jaw as if to hurt her in some way.

He nodded but did not comment on the conversation going on around him, while he waited to see what Lord Remmick would do next. So the rumors were true. Charlotte was in a marriage of the worst kind. If Lord Remmick was willing to grab his wife in public, one shuddered to think of what the man could do behind closed doors.

A simmering anger boiled in his blood at the thought of his childhood friend Charlotte, this beautiful woman she had grown into, being a punching bag for her husband's woes and disappointments.

It was not to be borne.

Mason downed the last of his brandy and strolled toward Charlotte and her husband. He couldn't help but smile when she stood, her large eyes full of welcome and also, he noted, apprehension.

He bowed. "Good evening, Lord and Lady Remmick. It has been a long time."

Charlotte curtsied. "Good evening, Lord Helsing. Indeed it has been a long time. Too long in fact."

Mason looked at Lord Remmick and waited for him to stand and acknowledge him. With a sigh of annoyance, he did so, swaying before Charlotte clasped his arm to keep him from falling over.

"Lord Helsing. We are honored by your presence. Why, I do believe the last time I saw you, you were quite put out." Lord Remmick laughed and splashed some of his water over his shirt. Not that it made any difference, as his lordship's shirt was already marred with stains of suspicious origins.

Mason cast Lord Remmick a dismissive glance and turned his attention back to Charlotte. She was as beautiful as he remembered her and yet something about her had changed. No longer did she seem as carefree and at ease as she once had. The spark that had glowed in her eyes was no longer there. No doubt, due to the fiend she'd married.

"Would you care to dance, my lady? There is to be a cotillion next."

Charlotte smiled. "I would love to, my lord."

"You would love to, my dear?" Remmick said, glaring at her. "What else would you love to do, I wonder? Were you not friends many years ago? And did I not steal her away from under your nose, Lord Helsing? You know my offer still stands."

Mason ground his teeth. Nothing would please him more than to punch the obnoxious bastard on his nose. Another time, he promised himself. "On the contrary, my lord. But you are right with one point. Lady Remmick and myself have known each other all our lives."

"What was the offer, James?" Charlotte asked, frowning.

Mason glared at his lordship, letting him know without words he should keep his mouth shut.

Remmick laughed. "I merely offered to share you, my dear. Of course, Lord Helsing would have to pay for your services. Not," he added, flicking a piece of invisible lint from his coat, "that you are worth very much. Your...abilities shall we say behind closed doors are somewhat...lacking."

Charlotte gasped and turned to walk away. Mason clasped her hand and pulled her onto the floor to dance with him instead. He looked down at her and anger churned in his stomach at her unshed tears.

"How are you, really, Charlotte?" he asked.

"Mortified. I cannot believe James could speak of me, or to you, in that unseemly manner. I'm so sorry."

"Don't be," he said, stepping away from her for a moment before the music brought them back together. "It is not your fault Lord Remmick is a cad. I apologize as he's your husband, but some things are better left unsaid."

Charlotte nodded and a pang of regret pierced Mason's soul. He regretted that he hadn't fought harder for her. Regretted that he hadn't insisted that her father break the contracts and damn the scandal. How could such a beautiful woman, inside and out, be married to the worst debaucher and rake in London.

"I have been watching you for a while and to me you do not have the appearance of a happy woman. Tell me everything is well at home?"

Charlotte paled and missed a step. Mason clasped her about her waist and a longing to hold her assailed him. "Please," he added.

She sighed. "We are perfectly well, thank you. There is nothing for you to worry about."

Mason's gut clenched at the lie. He watched her dance, and although she knew the song well, there was no joy in her eyes. No life.

"You're lying."

Charlotte met his gaze and Mason knew instinctively what type of life she lived. The bastard bashed her. Probably took pleasure in her pain. And she was frightened. This dance with him would probably make Lord Remmick think he had the right to hit her again.

"Truly, my lord. I'm fine. Please do not concern yourself." She cast a nervous glance to where her husband sat and frowned a little.

Mason looked over his shoulder and noted his lordship watching them intently. His visage one of fury. Mason ground his teeth. "You cannot stay married to him," he said. "He'll end up killing you, Charlotte and you know it. You must speak to your father at once."

"Shush," she said, looking about. "I've already told you there is nothing wrong. Now please, let us enjoy what's left of our dance, so we may part as friends."

"I can protect you." Mason gave her a pointed stare that dared her to refute him.

"You can protect me? How? By bringing shame and scandal to both our families? I'm married and there is nothing to be done."

Mason watched her storm from the dance floor just as the music ended. He sighed and looked about for her friend Lady Furrow. Spying her ladyship beside her husband, the Earl, Mason went to join them and to see what exactly could be done to save Charlotte from Lord Remmick and his abusive clutches.

# A GENTLEMAN'S PROMISE

Later that night, Charlotte sat on her bed and nursed the stinging slap James had bestowed on her cheek. It was a relief that his anger over her dancing with Lord Helsing had ended there. On the carriage ride home, he had chastised her endlessly, berated and yelled at her over her 'wantonness' and 'whoring' that, according to him, all of London knew and was talking about.

Sometimes Charlotte actually thought that James was losing his mind. Since their marriage, she'd been nothing but the best wife to him. A wife who tolerated a lot. Not that she had a choice in the matter. There was little anyone could do to make her situation improve.

She heard the front door slam and knew James had left for the night and if anything like his other nights out on town, wouldn't be home for several days. Charlotte rang for some heated water and waited. She sat before her dressing table and stared at her reflection. At twenty years, she was still an attractive woman.

Anger thrummed through her over her husband's violent behavior. Who was he to hit her? And why should she put up with it any longer? The next time he went to strike her would be his last.

Mason's words whispered in her mind, "I can protect you". There was no doubt that he could if she asked him. But other than divorcing Lord Remmick – which she refused to do – there was little to be done. Although, perhaps Mason could help her in another way. In the ways of a man and woman and in one need in particular.

Charlotte pulled the pins from her hair and let her light locks pool about her shoulders. Her dark cobalt blue eyes gave her an air of exoticness that she liked and from the glances which some gentleman had bestowed upon her, she knew that they appreciated her too.

She started when her maid brought in the water and towels. Charlotte dismissed her for the night. She washed thoroughly, then went to her armoire and looked through her clothing. She pulled out a gown that buttoned up at the front and had a hood. It was not something she would normally wear in public, but it was perfect for what she had planned in a certain gentleman's bedroom.

Searching through her chest of drawers she found an almost transparent shift and pulled it over her head. Then picking up the gown, she tied it up over the shift.

Nerves fluttered in her stomach over what she was about to do. Charlotte took a calming breath, pulled the hood over her hair and left her room. Walking down the stairs, she saw the night footman jump to attention as he noticed her and bowed.

"Can I help you, my lady?"

"Can you summon a hackney carriage please? I'm going out."

The footman nodded and ran outside. Charlotte pushed down the desire to run back to her room and forget the folly she'd embarked upon. Then, the thought of her husband and his abusiveness toward her strengthened her resolve. James could very well kill her the next time he was inclined to strike her. She'd be damned she'd die without living first.

The footman came in some minutes later and beckoned her toward the door. Charlotte followed him and took a calming breath of London's still night air. She gave the driver the direction to Lord Helsing's residence and sat back. Excitement over the unknown made her restless and she fidgeted with her reticule.

Would Mason admit her? By his hooded, appreciative

gaze during their dance tonight and his reassuring words she felt that he would. Still, she was married and what she was about to do was an unforgivable transgression. Charlotte supposed she should feel guilty, but all she felt was expectation. Like her body was alive again.

The drive was short and before Charlotte knew it, the cab pulled up beside a Georgian townhouse on Berkeley Square. Lights blazed from a first floor window and two from the second. Until now, she hadn't thought that Mason may still be out or worse, that he may be entertaining someone else... She pushed the dismal thought aside and stepped out onto the pavement. Paying the driver she walked up the short flight of steps and knocked.

Within moments a footman opened the door. His widened eyes told of his shock at seeing a lady dressed in hooded, secretive apparel and standing on the street in the middle of the night. Charlotte walked past him and into the foyer. The home was of similar layout to hers. With a tiled mosaic floor and winding staircase up to the second story, she could almost picture herself back there. Except this home, seemed much more comforting and welcoming than hers ever would.

"I'm here to see, Lord Helsing. Tell him Charlotte King is here. He isn't expecting me."

"If you'll wait here, Miss King."

Charlotte watched as the footman walked toward what she assumed to be the library or front drawing room. She heard muffled voices before rapid footsteps sounded in the adjacent room.

"Charlotte, are you well?" Lord Helsing clasped her hand and studied her for a moment. "What are you doing here?"

"May we speak in private, my lord?"

He frowned and Charlotte could read the confusion in his gaze. "Of course," he said. "Please, follow me."

The room was a library with floor to ceiling paneling and books. The smell of leather and cigars mixed with an old book scent Charlotte had always loved met her senses. She sat down on the settee before the unlit hearth and wondered for a moment if she'd done the right thing.

Pushing back her hood, she watched Mason shut and lock the door before joining her on the chair. Nerves skittered up her arm when he clasped her hand.

"He's hit you hasn't he? And don't lie to me this time. I can see by your reddened cheek that he has."

Charlotte nodded. "He's often violent and cruel. So cruel it's beyond imagining." Tears threatened to spill down her cheeks and she bit her lip. "I should never have married him. Had I known..."

"You weren't to know. I knew he was fond of nightly pursuits in the bowels of London, but I did not know he would hit his wife." He rubbed a tear from her cheek and Charlotte leaned toward his touch. It had been so long since she'd had contact filled with reverence and care with another person. "I should have waited. Married someone else. Anyone but James." She met his gaze and for the life of her, couldn't look away.

"I blame your father as much as I blame your husband. I have not told you this before but the day I came to visit your home, the day after we'd met at the lake I went there for a particular reason."

"Which was?" Charlotte asked frowning. Lord Helsing stood and went to stand before the hearth, watching as the flames licked at the wood. "I lied when I said I hadn't heard of your betrothal. I had. And having heard I set off for home to discuss the matter with your father. I knew of Lord Remmick's...history and thought to warn your father.

Make him see the error in agreeing for you to marry such a cad and therefore break the understanding." Mason paused and a pained expression crossed his visage. "He wouldn't listen." He turned and met her gaze. "I failed you that day. As a friend, a neighbor and as a gentleman."

"You didn't fail me, Mason," she said, using his Christian name for the first time in an age. "I failed myself." Tears pricked her eyes and she sniffed. "When father said you'd come with reservations about Lord Remmick I should have listened. I've know you for so long. We'd played, laughed, fought in the past but you've never placed me in harm's way. I should've taken heed of your doubt and acted on it."

"We all make mistakes, Charlotte. We wouldn't be human if we did not." He came and sat beside her and clasped her hand. "Why are you really here, Charlotte? It's the middle of the night."

A myriad of desires and needs thrummed through her veins at his direct question. Why was she here? Because she'd always loved him. From the moment she'd met him as a young girl, she'd loved him. Charlotte studied Mason's features, his straight nose and aristocratic jaw. His untidy hair that looked as if he'd run his fingers through it too many times. How she loved him.

Charlotte leaned forward and clasped his jaw. He stilled for a moment but didn't pull back as she continued on her quest and kissed him.

When he didn't respond, she sat back and studied his reaction. "I'm sorry. I don't know what I'm doing. I came here tonight to teach James a lesson and all I've ended up doing is making myself look like a fool." She swallowed a sob and searched for a handkerchief in her cloak pocket. She was a ridiculous fool, about to make another mistake to add to her many. Mason was her friend, not a lover.

Why she even thought he would look at her in that way was an absurd notion.

"You need to go home, Charlotte and think about what you wish to do. You're married and if we go down this road, there will be no turning back. For me at least," Mason said, standing and pulling her up. Her cloak opened and she quickly tied it closed again, but not before Mason had seen what scandalous evening wear she had on.

"I understand and you're right. Revenge is never the way to solve a problem, even my problems, as great as they are. I apologize for intruding upon you."

He clasped her jaw and made her look up at him. "I've always cared for you, you know that. Yes, many years passed that we never saw one another, but you were always thought of and wondered about. Do not imagine the reason I'm sending you home stems from my not wanting you. Without a second thought, I would rip that cloak from your shoulders, untie your shift and take you here on this settee and let your husband be damned. But I will not. If you want to be with me it needs to be out of your desire to be with me, not your lust to hurt your husband in any way you can."

Mason led Charlotte out of his townhouse and walked her though his back garden toward the mews. He summoned his stableman to fetch a Hackney and have the cab brought around the back.

"Pull your hood over your hair a little more, Charlotte. I don't want you to be seen leaving my premises." Mason looked toward the street and cursed the blasted Hackney driver for taking his time. Under the moonlight and knowing Charlotte wanted to sleep with him was almost too much to resist.

Almost…

But the thought that she would add him to her list of mistakes kept him rooted to the spot. She needed to come to him out of desire, need or affection…for him alone. But never revenge. He couldn't stomach that.

A tear slid down her cheek and he clamped his jaw. Damn it, he'd never intended to hurt her. The last person on earth he'd ever wish to injure was Charlotte. He pulled her into his arms.

Her willowy figure sat snug against his and he breathed in deep the exotic smell of her hair. "I don't send you away because I want to," he said, rubbing her back and knowing her body was only two pieces of material away. "Please say you understand."

The sound of the coach rumbled on the cobbled drive and Mason pulled Charlotte toward the gate. "Charlotte?"

She nodded and pulled back. "I do. I'm just mortified I humiliated myself."

Mason ran a hand through his hair. "You didn't. Just promise me you'll sleep on what I've said tonight. When you wake in the morning, you'll understand where I'm coming from. But know this, it isn't due to my lack of interest."

She nodded. "Goodnight, Lord Helsing."

Mason helped her into the coach and shut the door. He flicked the driver a sovereign and gave the man Charlotte's address. "Goodnight, my lady," he said as he watched it drive away before turning a corner and going out of view. He swore and stormed back through his garden gate and strode toward his house. For the first time in his life, Mason cursed the fact he'd been born a gentleman and given the airs of one. Next time, he wasn't quite sure he would have it in him to deny Charlotte anything.

Least of all himself.

## CHAPTER 7

Mason sat atop his horse and watched as Charlotte galloped down Rotten Row at breakneck speed. A week had passed since he'd seen her, her avoidance of him starting to irritate. The fact she was also out riding without a chaperone grated on his nerves. Since kissing her, as quick and innocent as that kiss was, Mason had cursed his gentlemanly behavior. His gut clenched at the memory and he swore.

Charlotte, un-chaperoned and alone, wasn't safe, not with him around at least.

He cantered toward her and watched as her eyes flared in surprise. "Good morning, Lady Remmick," he said, tipping his head in acknowledgement.

A shade of rose bloomed on her cheeks and he smiled. "Lord Helsing," she replied. "I thought I had this turf to myself this morning, being as early as I am."

"I like to ride early myself. It clears my head." She looked about and shifted on her saddle and Mason wondered what she was thinking. Was she uncomfortable around him now? Did she regret her words and actions of a week earlier? "I have not seen you about. I hope you're well."

"I'm very well, thank you, my lord. The weather is very congenial today, my horse…"

Mason ground his teeth at the benign banter. He sighed. "Charlotte, if we're only ever going to speak about the weather or our horses, our conversation will soon bore even me. And while I like to discuss my cattle as much as any other gentleman, I do wish you would trust me enough to talk to me as a friend."

A pained expression flitted across her features. "I cannot. I'm sorry."

"Yes you can, you just don't want to." He threw her a pointed stare. "Charlotte?" Again she looked about before she met his gaze and raised her chin.

"I'm so sorry about last week. I really don't know what came over me. I'm not usually like that." She bit her lip and his gut clenched. "Please forgive me."

"There is nothing to forgive. You've done nothing wrong. If anything, it is I who owe you an apology."

"Why?" she asked.

"For turning you away."

Charlotte's stomach twisted into delightful knots at Mason's words. For days, she'd chastised herself for a silly fool. Embarrassment over how she'd propositioned him made her squirm daily. Never did she think she could look him in the eye again without dying on the spot. But the gentleman that Mason was, proved her wrong. He read her as easily as a book and knew her reaching out for him was just that. A call to help and comfort when she was down. The fact that he didn't take advantage of her during a time of need spoke volumes as to what kind of man he was.

He was a true gentleman. "I understand why you did and I thank you for doing so. I so wish for us to be friends again. To be as close as we were as children. I've always thought of you and hoped you were happy." Charlotte walked her horse on and smiled when he came abreast. "Tell me about Bath and your time there. When time permits, I really should make a trip up there myself. I have a cousin who lives there did you know?"

"I do know that, yes," he said. "I enjoy travelling and although Bath is not so very far away, the limited society suits me. I'll return there should the season in town prove…"

"Prove what?" Charlotte asked, wondering why Mason looked uncomfortable for the first time since she'd seen him. "Mason, what were you going to say?"

He chuckled. "Prove disappointing. I find now that I'm nearing thirty I should look for a wife if you really must know."

"How diverting," Charlotte said laughing and enjoying herself for the first time in a very long time. "No one caught your fancy? I find that very hard to believe."

"Believe it, my lady for it is true. And not through lack of trying on my behalf. But there was never that…"

"Spark?" Charlotte smiled at him and he nodded.

"Yes, that spark," he replied catching her eye.

Charlotte knew all too well what that spark felt like and to know you were married to a man who didn't raise so much as a flicker of a flame left her hollow. Not to mention that after that fleeting kiss she'd shared with Mason, her whole outlook on love and what a man and woman could share with mutual desire, had altered. For the first time since she'd watched him swim in the lake, she'd desired a man to touch her. To do more than just kiss her. She'd wanted him. Desperately. And none of the emotions resembled revenge. When she thought of passion, she thought of only Mason and not her husband.

"I hope you find it, my lord. There is nothing worse, believe me, than to live a life without that spark."

Mason sighed and pulled his horse to a stop as other riders took to the track just ahead of them. "I do not wish that for you, Charlotte. You're a beautiful woman. A kind and considerate lady who deserves so much more than you've been dealt. Ask me again."

Charlotte shivered at his words and met his gaze. "Ask you what again?" Her voice came out in a rush and she inwardly swore. As if she didn't know just what.

"Ask me."

Mason's voice resonated with steadfast resolve and she tore her gaze away from his. To think straight, she couldn't drown in orbs so blue and swirling with need that she would flounder. But how could she not wade out into murky waters? Not to would mean never to live, experience all that life, this man, was offering her.

"You didn't want me to ask unless it wasn't owing to my seeking revenge," she stated.

"Then make sure it does not. Now ask."

"Will you sleep with me?" The words came out as a rushed whisper, but Mason heard. A muscle on his temple worked as he stared silently at her.

"I don't believe sleep will factor into our agreement, my lady."

Were it possible Charlotte's toes would've curled in her boots. "I hope not."

CHAPTER 8

Charlotte settled against the squabs of her hackney cab and tried to calm her nerves. After meeting Mason in Hyde Park the thought of what they were about to start, to do with each other left excitement thrumming through her veins and expectation right alongside of it. It had taken three days for James to leave. The reason why he could be staying home annoyed and worried her at the same time. Not that she cared what happened to her husband anymore, that part of her conscience had died a long time ago, but maybe he'd caught some awful disease and was sick. And should he force himself on her would make her sick also. She shuddered and tried to calm her racing thoughts. Tonight she needed to concentrate on one man and one man only.

Mason.

The cab pulled up before his town house and she alighted and was ushered inside without having to knock. She smiled and walked toward the library having seen the candlelight flickering from the ajar door.

Mason sat leaning on his knees and staring at the

44

flames in the hearth. He looked lost in thought, even worried if the slight frown lines beside his eyes were any indication. Charlotte stopped and wondered if he'd changed his mind. Regretted his words.

*Please no.*

"My Lord?"

Mason stood quickly and came over to greet her. He smiled as he reached over her shoulder and shut the door. "Good evening, my lady."

Charlotte handed him her cloak and laughed. "I'm so nervous. I know I shouldn't be, because you'd never hurt me, but I've never done…"

"Come and sit." He pulled her toward the settee and her hand burned at his touch. She had wondered over the last few days if that spark they spoke of was a figment of imagination, need, on her behalf. But now, right at this moment, with his large hand clamped around hers, she knew such thoughts were untrue. With Mason her whole body reacted, sparked to life like a firecracker ready to explode.

She sat.

"You're very beautiful this evening." Mason ran a finger down her cheek, leaned in and kissed beneath her ear. Charlotte shut her eyes and bit her lip to stop herself from throwing herself into his arms like a crazed, affection starved matron.

"Thank you," she managed.

His lips touched her shoulder and she shivered. "There is no need for thanks."

She clutched the lapels of his coat and pulled him against her. "Mason. Please."

He growled and took her lips in a searing kiss. Finally!

Charlotte moaned as his tongue licked her lips. Heat coursed through her veins when he deepened the embrace;

almost consuming her with his desire. Never had she wanted anyone as much as she wanted Mason to take her here, right now, on his library settee.

"Are you sure?" he said, clasping her hand when it reached the buttons on his frontfalls.

"I have never been more certain of anything." Again, her lips touched his while her hand unbuttoned his breeches. It took some coaxing to slip open his buttons, but eventually the flap opened and she was able to clasp his straining member.

Velvety, soft skin slid against her palm and Mason moaned. Charlotte wrapped her fingers about him and stroked him as he kissed her senseless. Heat pooled at her core and she gasped when his hand kneaded her breast through her dress.

"I want you," she managed to say. Mason quickly unbuttoned the front of her dress, pushing the garment from her shoulders. He pulled back for a moment to pull her transparent shift over her head, leaving her naked.

Cool night air kissed her skin and Charlotte felt her nipples peak into tight buds. She bit her lip at the savagery and desire she could read in his gaze as it locked on her, scorched her. Expectation ran up her spine and she ran her hand over the tip of his penis feeling his desire.

He laid her down onto the settee and settled between her legs. Charlotte gasped as he pushed against her sex and teased her with his body. Her breathing hitched as he watched and continued to taunt her relentlessly.

"I won't want to give you back, Charlotte. There is no denying me if we do this. From this moment on, you're mine and no other's."

Her mind a haze, Charlotte nodded. Would in fact do anything Mason said right at this moment. He pushed a little inside and started to pay homage to her breasts. She ran her fingers through his dark locks and held him there. The wicked things he was doing with his tongue sent sensations to spike toward her core. "Mason please," she begged.

He chuckled and feathered kisses up her neck before kissing her lips with such reverence that Charlotte could almost defy any scandal to come live with him. Divorce James and marry Lord Helsing indeed.

"You are mine." The deep, lust-tinged voice brooked no argument as he thrust into her core and took her. "Always," he said.

She gasped as the size of him took her a moment to accommodate. Fullness and completeness was all she felt. Charlotte wrapped her legs about his waist and a delicious pressure built inside. She clutched at his shoulders and realized with some amusement that he still wore his shirt and pants. The image of her naked and Mason above her, taking her fully clothed made her moan.

"Mason, I'm—"

"Let go, Charlotte."

She met his gaze and bit her lip. Oh, it felt so good. Tighter and tighter she coiled about him, needing to be closer, wanting him harder with every stroke, until a pleasure unlike any she thought possible exploded in and all around her.

"Mason," she moaned into his shoulder. Her body riding his until the last of her orgasm was spent. Mason quickened his pace, his gasp against her ear marking his own orgasm.

They stayed like that for a time, both trying to regain their breath and understanding over what had just happened between them.

Charlotte pulled back and pushed a lock of hair from his face. "That was amazing."

He chuckled. "Yes it was," he said, kissing her again, in a slow, sensuous manner. "And I meant what I said before, Charlotte. I'll not share you."

Charlotte swallowed. "I'm married, Mason. You have to accept that."

The moment he pulled away, she missed his heat. He stood and walked toward the hearth, and Charlotte could tell by the tautness of his shoulders that he was angry. And he had every right to be. But then, he knew why she'd come here for tonight. To seek solace, love from a man she'd always admired and cared for. They were just two people who had freely chosen to love each other. Nothing more could be between them other than friendship and perhaps a repeat of tonight, if he was willing. But no matter how much she wished to divorce James, she could not. The scandal would kill her father, not to mention ruin her sister's hope of marrying well.

Mason ran a hand through his hair. "You deserve better, Charlotte. Leave him and be damned the scandal."

Charlotte came over and clasped his hands. "I know you would support me should I do such a thing. You're the best of men, but I cannot. I don't care about my own reputation, but should I leave James I'd ruin my sister in an instant. My parents would never recover from the shock."

"Do they know how violent James is? Surely your father would not wish you to come to any harm."

"Of course he wouldn't, but no they do not." Charlotte stepped away and started to look for her gown. "He may be cross and talk to James but that would only ensure another beating for me at his hands. I'm married and that is that."

"It's not that." The vehemence behind Mason's tone sent shivers up Charlotte's spine.

She pulled on her dress and started doing up its

buttons. "I know I'm being selfish in wanting you without any recourse or commitment. In fact you may think me fast, a woman best suited for the *demi monde* than the society we grace. But I just wanted you. I've wanted you for so long it, physically hurt." Charlotte took a calming breath. "Let us have some time together, please. If my sister marries then I will leave James as soon as the ink is dry on the marriage register."

Mason stared at her a moment then came and pulled her into his arms. He smelt divine, of sandalwood and her. Charlotte snuggled into his chest and reveled in the beat of his heart.

"So, we're to have a repeat performance of tonight? You are wanton, Charlotte."

She laughed the sound almost foreign to her. "With you I am, my lord. When can I see you again?"

"Are you attending Lord and Lady Wilson's ball tomorrow evening?"

Charlotte nodded, having received the invitation to London's most looked forward to event. Every year his lordship always threw a ball where something happened. Whether it be a betrothal, a performance or special guest, Lord Wilson always had something to keep his guests occupied and happy.

"So? We will speak then."

Charlotte leaned up and kissed him quickly. "I shall miss you."

He growled and swooped her into his arms. "Who said I was ready to let you go?" And he didn't let her go; not until the hour before dawn.

## CHAPTER 9

Charlotte couldn't wipe away the smile from her lips as she watched Lord Helsing stroll across the room toward her. Tonight he wore a blue, superfine, long tailed coat with a pristine white shirt and waistcoat beneath. His neckcloth was tied perfectly and only accentuated his handsome visage, very much like his black satin knee-breeches that fit his masculine thighs to perfection. He looked regal and tall, a gentleman with a roguish grin that left her knees weak.

She swallowed as heat coursed throughout her body, remembering what he'd done to her the night before. After seeing him as a man at her father's lake all those years ago, Charlotte had often wondered what he'd be like when intimate with a woman. And now she knew and was anything but disappointed with her findings.

As luck would have it, her husband was still absent since his departure the previous evening, and so tonight, Charlotte was here by herself. Of course, Amelia waltzed about the floor with Lord Furrow, but no longer did she feel the need to impinge on the happily married couple's time. At least not as much as she'd formerly done.

For now, she had another more fascinating companion. Lord Helsing.

"Good evening, Lady Remmick. May I say how beautiful you look this evening?"

The devilish twinkle in Mason's gaze made goosebumps rise across her flesh. Charlotte tapped her fan against his arm and curtsied. "Good evening, my lord."

He came and stood beside her with his hands behind his back before he leaned in and whispered against her ear, "May I also say how delicious you look, Charlotte. Good enough to eat, in fact."

Charlotte refused to blush and instead laughed to cover her nervousness. "Behave." She met his gaze and the heat she read in his eyes made her breath hitch in her lungs.

"I don't want to."

How could just four simple words leave her aching with need? She had, after all only left his bed in the early hours of this morning. And yet, here she was, panting like she'd run about the block in a tightly strung corset. "Then we're in agreement. Although the thing is, my lord," Charlotte said moving closer to his side to ensure privacy, "what are we to do about it?"

Mason took two flutes of champagne from a passing footman and handed one to Charlotte. "Well that is yet to be decided. But I can imagine one thing we'd both enjoy immensely."

Charlotte laughed and took a cooling sip of her drink. "Later?"

He nodded and excitement thrummed in her veins. Were she not married, her urge to clasp his arm and declare to everyone present that he was hers would have been beyond her control. Charlotte pushed away the depressing thought that he wasn't hers and instead turned her attention to the guests at the ball.

The musicians played an elegant piece of music while the dancers moved gracefully about the floor, partaking in conversations before their dance began. Wax candles in crystal chandeliers ran the length of the room and basked everyone in a forgiving light, giving the room an air of mystery.

"Would you care to dance, Charlotte?"

She smiled but shook her head. "You should dance with someone else. People will talk if you show too much inclination toward me."

He shrugged. "Let them talk."

At her raised brow, he growled and downed the last of his champagne before stepping away from her and moving about the room with casual elegance. Every step reminded her of a large cat searching for its next victim. Yet no one could be a victim when it came to Mason. Never had she known a better man than Lord Helsing. And after her marriage with James and meeting the friends he frequented the gambling dens with, she wondered if she could count on her fingers how many good men she knew, in truth.

Mason walked toward the card room and slipped out of Charlotte's sight lest she make him dance with a green country girl ripe for the picking. He looked about the room and spying his friend, George Lord Mountbatten playing piquet, joined him.

"Helsing," his friend said, clapping him on the shoulder. "Good to see you." George gestured to the gentleman sitting across from him. "You remember Sir Phillip Penry?"

Mason nodded and sat. "Of course," he said as he

watched George play for a moment before he won the hand with a flurry of excitement.

Sir Penry pushed back his chair and stood. "Well that's me done for the night. I'll leave you gentleman to it, shall I?"

George laughed and started to slide his winnings toward himself. "Come man, the night's still early. You never know, I may have a bad round and you could win all your blunt back."

"Lord Mountbatten have a bad round?" Sir Penry scoffed. "That is something I shall never see."

Mason laughed. "How many good men have you fleeced tonight, George?"

"A few," his oldest friend said, sitting back and lighting a cigar. "What brings you in here? Are you running away from the maiden debutantes that are nipping at every gentleman's heels hoping for a marriage proposal?"

The thought of Charlotte and her anything but debutantes nipping assailed Mason's mind and he shifted in his seat. "No. Not a debutante."

George whistled and leaned forward. "Who is she? Do I know her?"

Mason debated telling his most trusted friend for only a moment. George would never disclose his secret and bring censure down on Charlotte. "Lady Remmick," he said, without ceremony. George's shock was clearly visible before he composed himself with a gulp of brandy.

"She's married."

"I know," Mason said, stemming the urge to roll his eyes. "But..."

"What?"

"I want her. I think I've wanted her a lot longer than I would admit to even myself." Mason rubbed his jaw and met George's stunned gaze. It wasn't often he could confound his friend, but on this occasion he had.

"Lord Remmick will never let her go. He's not a man I'd wish to cross. You'd better be certain Lady Remmick is worth—"

"She is," he said, cutting him off. "You've seen the bastard. He whores around worse than the women walking the streets in Drury Lane. And it's only a matter of time before he kills Charlotte either by disease or force."

"He's violent?"

Mason nodded. "Yes. Often. Charlotte says he loses his temper over the simplest things and no matter what anyone says or does, there is no stopping his rage. He's unbalanced, to say the least."

"What are you going to do?" George asked, summoning a footman for more drinks.

"Charlotte wants to keep it a simple, secretive affair. But how can I let her go home and share her with that bastard?"

George shook his head and sighed. "You'll have to. Until Lady Remmick is ready to leave his lordship and face the fall from grace she undoubtedly will, you can do nothing. My advice is to enjoy your liaison. It's been too long since you've had one."

A shiver of unease rippled down Mason's back and looking over his shoulder, he spied Lord Remmick glaring at him from the gaming room door.

Mason turned back to George and swore. "The bastard's here."

"I noticed. And what's more, he's coming this way."

Mason braced himself for the forthcoming confrontation with his lordship. His skin crawled when Charlotte's husband slumped into the chair across from him and smirked.

"Gentlemen," Lord Remmick said, the smell of spirits and sex emanating off his breath and clothes.

Mason fought not to cringe. "Lord Remmick," he drawled. "To what do we owe the pleasure?"

"Come Lord Helsing. Or should I call you Mason, as my delightful whore of a wife does?"

Mason noted George visibly stiffened at the insult to Lady Remmick. Mason shrugged lest he clasp the bastard about the neck and strangle him. "You may call me whatever you choose. But call Lady Remmick, your wife should I remind you, a whore once more and I'll make sure you cannot speak another word for a week.

Lord Remmick grinned and pulled out a container of snuff. "You owe me."

Mason raised his brow. "What for?"

"For fucking my wife, of course. You should know there is nothing that Charlotte does that I do not know about. And last night she left our home and did not return until the early hours of this morning. The way you watch her, pant at her flesh like a dog in heat makes it easy for me to know it was you she visited."

"Really?" Mason took a sip of brandy and wondered who in Charlotte's household was spying on her. Not to mention the thought that she could possibly be beaten later tonight by this blight on society made his blood boil. "Prove it."

"Ah, but you see that I cannot do. Perhaps not this time at least. Even so, I want five-hundred pounds delivered to White's in my name by tomorrow lunch." Lord Remmick smirked. "And don't delay."

"I will not. Wherever Lady Remmick went last night it was not to me," Mason lied. "So you may keep your requests for funds to yourself. Perhaps you ought to ask Lady Remmick's herself for blunt if you're so short. She was the one, after all, who brought all the money back into your family name."

Charlotte's husband's face mottled red in anger. Mason relished the sight, wanting to strike at him in any way he could. But never would he disclose to this bastard what Charlotte and himself had done. He had made love to her, and no man, not even the pathetic specimen of manhood before him would mar his memory.

"Touch her again and I'll ruin you."

Mason laughed. "You'll ruin me? A man already ruined by his vices of hard living and drinking? Should you spread such vicious lies about London, you'll not only hurt Lady Remmick ,but yourself. Don't be a fool."

His lordship stood and clasped the table for support as he swayed. "Five hundred. Not a penny short," he said, before leaving.

Mason met George's worried visage and inwardly groaned.

"He knows."

"So it would seem," Mason said, thinking over what he could do and coming up blank. "He can't prove anything. And there is not an iota of a chance of me paying him a penny. I'll not let Lord Remmick make Charlotte into his prostitute."

"You'll have to be careful from now on," George said. "Lord Remmick will be watching her like a hawk now that he thinks he can gain funds from her nightly pursuits. And if that fails, he's likely to challenge you to a duel."

Mason drank down the last of his wine and pushed back his chair. "Lord Remmick will be lucky if I do not challenge him. And I will ensure that Charlotte's reputation is safe from scandal," he said, walking back toward the ballroom.

He found Charlotte standing beside Lady Furrow, her

puckered brow and pale countenance indicative of her recent encounter with her husband. Anger thrummed through Mason's body and an urge to come across Lord Remmick in a darkened ally had never sounded more desirable.

He bowed as he came to stand before them and smiled at Charlotte who didn't seem to be the jovial woman he'd left, not a half hour before. "Would you care for a stroll, Lady Remmick?" He kept his gaze on Charlotte and waited for her to decide. She bit her lip and something in his gut clenched. Married or not, he was attracted to this woman like his lungs were to air. The need to make her happy, to be with her in any way he could, was like a drug to his system. "Charlotte," he prompted.

She cast a nervous glance at Lady Furrow, then nodded. "Of course."

Mason took her hand and placed it on his arm before moving toward the French doors leading out toward a lawn patio, overlooking the garden.

"Your husband arrived and sought you out, I see," he said, as they walked toward the corner of Lord Wilson's townhouse.

"Yes. He was here." She paused. "He wanted to know if I enjoyed myself last night."

Mason shook his head at the scum's audacity to ask such a question to his wife, especially given the way Lord Remmick lived his own life. Yet, a prick of guilt stabbed at Mason that he was being selfish wanting to continue the affair with Charlotte. But then the memory of her beaten black and blue from her husband pushed away such guilt. Lord Remmick didn't deserve her. And Mason wanted her and would have her, at any cost.

"What did you say?"

"That I did. And then Amelia, Lady Furrow, obviously

noting my husband's furious countenance said we'd had a delightful time at her home playing cards." Charlotte smiled. "James didn't know what to say or do. He left shortly after."

They slipped around the corner and the smell of London, the distant sounds of the city, echoed across the sky. The yard this side of the house encompassed a small pavilion covered in a rose climber and neat garden beds set out in symmetrical shapes with lawn between the beds for ease of walking. Mason pulled Charlotte closer to his side and walked them toward the private pavilion. This side of the house was shadowed, moonlight their only means of light.

Walking into the circular structure Mason noted no chairs only the railings which looked out onto the foliage about them. Charlotte stopped and looked up at him expectantly. He slipped a lock of her hair behind her ear and ran a hand down her nape, electing a shiver to course through her body. His own hardened before he leaned forward and kissed her.

She met his eagerness with one that matched and his breath hitched in his lungs. The feel of her tongue twining and mimicking his had him as hard as a rock within moments.

He spun her about and pushed her against the railing, then slowly lifted her gown from behind. From here should anyone look, they would only see a couple taking in the garden around them and nothing more. Not a man who was about to take a woman up against a garden structure and enjoy every delicious, sensuous moment of it.

"Mason, what are you doing?" she asked, gasping when he slipped his finger to run around her stockinged thigh.

"Seducing you. I want you," he said feathering kisses

across the back of her neck. Charlotte didn't say anything, just pushed against his straining cock and Mason had his answer. He strained against his breeches and closed his eyes when her hand came behind and clasped him through the material.

Untying the frontfalls quickly, he lifted her skirt and stepped further between her legs. His cock strained for release yet the urge to tease Charlotte, make her want him as much as he did, made him rein in his baser needs.

He slipped a finger into her hot, wet passage and fought for control when she tightened about him. "You're so sweet, Charlotte," he said, kissing her neck while he kneaded her breast with his free hand. "I'm going to make you come."

"Yes." Charlotte rode his finger and undulated in his arms like a woman beyond thought. Mason removed his finger and stroked his phallus against her sex. She gasped and lifted her arms to clasp him about his nape.

"Please," she whispered, hardly audible.

"What, darling," he said, slipping a little inside of her before rubbing once more against her sex. "Tell me what you want."

"You." She tried to move and impale herself on his shaft and Mason bit down on a groan before continuing to tease them both senseless.

"I want you. All of you."

Unable to hold off any longer, Mason leaned Charlotte a little over the railing and slipped inside. Her hot core clasped tight about him and he felt a slight tremble course through her sex. "You're so close," he gasped, sheathing himself fully within her.

He held still for a moment and took a steadying breath less he spill himself before he'd brought her to orgasm. And then Charlotte shifted a little and started to ride him.

Mason's axis tilted. Never had he known a lady to act in such an erotic way before. He clasped her hips and guided her as she rode him from in front. His balls ached; in fact, his whole body ached for release. It was a heady experience indeed, being fucked by a woman in such a way. Yet not any woman, but Charlotte.

She made soft mewing sounds before her tempo changed, slowing down and riding his whole length. "You make me feel…"

"Let go, darling." Mason let her ride him and felt as the first contractions tightened about his shaft. She moaned into the cool night air and unable to stand the relentless torture of her orgasm that pulled at him, he joined her.

Lights blazed behind his eyelids as he emptied himself deep into her womb. "Charlotte," he said, gasping. "You're everything to me."

She let go of the railing and turned a little in his arms to look up at him. Her eyes shone bright in the moonlight and Mason hoped she could see from his own features just what she made him feel, what she was coming to mean to him.

"Am I?"

He lightly kissed her and pulled her hard against his chest. "Yes."

Her tentative smile warmed his blood. "I'm glad for I'd hate to be the only one here who feels this way."

Mason nodded. He knew exactly how she was feeling. Like a life was blossoming before them, like the roses climbing the pavilion in which they now stood. He would give her time to realize she had no future with Lord Remmick and then he would be there for her. But it would have to be her choice. Charlotte would face social ruin and – although an easy decision for him – Mason knew not so for a woman of class. But she would eventually leave the bastard. And when she did he'd be there to protect her. Marry her.

He kissed her again and let the embrace deepen into a firestorm of desire. In the interim, he'd ensure Lord Remmick and himself would have a little tête-à-tête.

Face to face.

In private.

M ason didn't have to wait long for his chance to talk to Lord Remmick. He stood in Drury Lane and watched as the bastard rutted like an animal with a whore from the streets. Her gasps of what sounded like pain making his lordship moan with pleasure.

The bastard was sick.

Mason waited for him to be finished then walked toward him, the whore walking quickly away and tying her gown as she did so.

"I hope I didn't make you rush, Lord Remmick."

His lordship started and looked up from tying his front-falls. "You didn't rush me, as the night is only young and I've plenty more of those whores yet to fuck." Lord Remmick took a sniff of snuff. "What do you want, Helsing? Permission to screw my wife?" Like I said earlier tonight, pay me the money tomorrow and I'll gladly give you her cunt."

Helsing punched the bastard and a fire in his stomach ignited as he watched him smack against the cobbled road.

"I should kill you now. No one would know." Helsing leaned over Charlotte's husband and kicked him in the balls for good measure. "Start treating your wife with respect or I'll hunt you down each and every time I see a new bruise on her face and I'll make sure you sport one a lot bigger and darker." He paused. "Do you understand?"

Remmick glared and wiped the blood from his nose. "You're a fool to care for her. She's the coldest, most uncaring woman I know. And she's married to me. You can never have her."

Helsing refused to react to the bastard's taunt. Charlotte was anything but what her husband proclaimed her to be. Never had he known a more caring, warm person in all his life. Why, the day they'd met as children was entirely due to her finding his lost wolfhound. She had been a girl full of life and immense chatter in those days, and she would be again one day, as soon as Mason rid her of her diseased and unhinged husband of hers. Freed her of a life of which she was no longer happy to be a part.

"Do you understand?" Mason repeated, kicking Lord Remmick in the stomach just for the sake of it.

Remmick sputtered and rolled onto his side. "I understand, Helsing. Now fuck off."

Mason smiled. "Gladly. Goodnight."

He walked away and summoning a hackney, headed back to Mayfair. As the cab pulled away he looked out and saw Remmick get on his feet and stagger off into the night. Unease crept down his spine and he hoped he hadn't just made Charlotte's life harder. That had never been his intention.

## CHAPTER 10

Charlotte walked into the foyer of her London home and watched as an array of luggage was piled at the base of the stairs by busy footmen. A moment later, her cousin, Rose from Bath walked serenely into the house and came toward her, a smile on her lips.

"Charlotte, it's so wonderful to see you again. You cannot believe how excited I am to be in the capital at last."

Charlotte kissed her cheek and noted her cousin's appearance and apparel. "And you, my dear." She looked toward the carriage and frowned when it pulled away from the curb. "Where is your mama? I thought she was to accompany you."

"She fell ill, unfortunately. Or perhaps, fortunately I should say. But that does not matter as I'm here now and you're married and able to chaperone me to all the balls and parties."

Charlotte started at this tidbit of information that she'd gone from having guests to stay to being a lady who sponsored a debutante about London. It was Rose's first

London season, due to Bath having been a disaster the year before. The poor girl had formed a tendre for a particular gentleman, who had hightailed off to London before asking Rose to marry him. Rose's mama, worrying about her daughter's future, had suggested London. A change in location was surely what was needed, to raise her daughter's spirits. And so here she was.

"Well, I hope Aunt May recovers soon. And of course I'll chaperone you. In fact, you'd better have your things unpacked and perhaps have a lie down before tonight. We're attending a masquerade."

"I'm not sure if mama would approve of me attending a mask, Charlotte. Are they not where trysts of the night occur?"

Charlotte laughed and hoped that *was* the case. Especially when it involved Mason and herself. She shook away the unhelpful thought. "Not the masquerade we're going to, my dear. But I will not lie to you, there are sections of society that partake in such risqué behavior, but I'm not one of them." The image of what she'd done the night before in the garden bombarded her mind and heat coursed up her neck.

"Are you well, Charlotte. You seem to have reddened. You're not blushing, surely?"

Charlotte laughed, covering up her discomfiture. "I'm fine dearest. Now, run along upstairs, I'll have a maid sent up to help you unpack and prepare you for tonight."

"Thank you," Rose said, kissing Charlotte's cheek. "I'm so grateful to you. I'm sure by the end of the season I'll be happily married like you and living probably across the park from this very house."

"I hope so too," Charlotte said, pushing her cousin toward the stairs. "And make sure you rest. That's an order."

Rose smiled. "I promise."

Later that evening, Charlotte stood beside Rose in a room full of the ton, some dressed in dominos and masks that completely concealed their identity. Others, like herself, wore an elaborate hair piece or half mask and regular gowns. Either way, the room was a kaleidoscope of color and elegance. Charlotte smiled at Rose and wondered if she too had looked like that three years ago, full of hopes and dreams, when she'd had her debut in London.

The memory of James and his elegance of courtship that had been a mask like the one she now wore, made her tremble with regret. How had she not sensed his rotten core? Rose clasped her arm and pulled her from her musings and Charlotte promised she wouldn't let her cousin suffer the same fate. She would have her marry for love and nothing less.

"He is here," Rose said.

Charlotte frowned and turned to her cousin. "Who is here, dearest?"

"The gentleman I wrote to you about. You know, the one who had to leave on urgent business in London just, before he could propose."

Charlotte refrained from mentioning to her young cousin that the gentleman's hightailing it to the capital could have been because an offer of marriage was expected. It was just like something James would do. Take his fill and then walk away without a backward glance, and not a blot on his conscience.

"Perhaps you could introduce me." Charlotte smiled at Rose and she nodded her eyes bright with excitement.

"I would like that," Rose said.

Charlotte turned her attention back to the guests, some dancing, others gambling and chatting in groups about the room. She spied Amelia and waved to her dearest friend who was dressed as a tavern wench, her bust almost spilling from her gown.

Feeling a prickling of desire across her skin, Charlotte looked toward the card room and spied Mason leaning casually against the door. He was dressed in a black superfine suit and black silk breeches. His waistcoat embroidered with intricate gold stitching matched his golden cravat. Never had she thought she'd react to a man like she did when he was present. Like her skin, her very being was attached to him in some way, reliant on him to keep her alive. Alive with desire and love.

"He's coming this way."

Charlotte tore her gaze from Mason and turned toward Rose as a sliver of dread ran up her spine. "You never told me the gentleman's name, Rose. Who was it that you formed an understanding with in Bath?"

Rose leaned toward her to enable privacy. "Lord Helsing from Somerset. Perhaps you know him as I understand his country estate resides not far from your parents' home."

Charlotte fought the bout of nausea that settled in her stomach. "Lord Helsing was the one from whom you expected an offer of marriage?"

Rose nodded. "Yes. He courted me most ardently in Bath and mama was sure he was in love with me. But then he just up and left, made an excuse to papa about urgent business in the capital."

*Urgent business.* Was she, Charlotte, the urgent business? She had wondered why all of a sudden he was back in town and seemingly courting her. Anger thrummed through her veins at the thought he'd used her cousin and now her. But that wasn't really the case, as Charlotte was the one who sought him out. Asked him to lie with her.

She watched him walk toward her and noticed his step faltered when he spied Rose standing beside her. Charlotte ground her teeth. What Rose had said was true. He'd courted her cousin and left her hanging like a ripe apple on a tree.

He continued on and bowed when he stopped before them. Charlotte held his gaze before she curtsied. "Lord Helsing, you know my cousin, Miss Rose Lancer of course."

Charlotte didn't miss the widening of his eyes at the manner of her introduction that held no warmth.

"Of course," he bowed. "It's a pleasure to see you again, Miss Lancer."

"Rose, please, Lord Helsing. We are acquainted well enough for you to use my given name."

"Perhaps in Bath, my dear but in London it is best to use your proper salutation." Charlotte glared at Mason and hoped he could read the fury over his behavior in her eyes. "My cousin was telling me about your time in Bath, my lord."

He nodded his eyes narrowing in suspicion. "Would you care to dance, Miss Lancer. For old times' sake."

"I would love to, thank you, my lord."

Charlotte smiled at Rose and watched as he led her cousin onto the floor. They did make a striking pair. She was fair and he was not. Both tall, yet perfectly proportioned for one another. Not to mention the fact that neither were married.

Despair threatened to make her ill. What was she doing? Having an affair with a man who could not save her. Only she could save herself and as much as Charlotte hated to admit it, she was too weak to leave. To throw society the biggest scandal of the year and divorce James like she should. But she could not. And here she was, angry at Lord Helsing, and all because last season, he had courted her cousin in Bath. Perhaps.

Granted having done so, he should have offered marriage. But had he really courted her or was Rose's attachment to him so strong that she desperately hoped his attention toward her was just that?

Charlotte turned away from the couples dancing a fast quadrille and went to find the ladies' retiring room. She slipped through a door and walked toward a footman who stood before a door near the end of the passageway. Tiredness swamped her and all she wished to do was leave.

"Charlotte!"

She whirled to find Mason storming toward her, his countenance one of frustration and concern.

"Where are you going?"

"Away from you." She continued past the footman and toward a door that seemed to lead outside. He followed her and she fought the urge to turn about and scold him in front of a servant.

The balmy night air kissed her skin as they stepped onto a darkened terrace. Charlotte continued on and heard Mason close the door behind them.

"Charlotte, stop."

She did and took a moment to calm down before he joined her. "I request that you leave me be."

"Don't be absurd. Why would I do that?"

She shrugged. "Oh, I don't know. Perhaps because you owe my cousin a proposal of marriage after you courted her last season."

"I never courted her. I was her friend and acquaintance, but that's all." He frowned and ran a hand through his hair. "She resembled you and I suppose I gravitated toward her because of that."

Charlotte stepped away from him. "You used her then, which is worse. How could you, Mason?"

A muscle ticked at his temple. "I apologize if it seems like I did, but I didn't do it intentionally. You did marry someone else, Charlotte."

"You didn't ask me to marry you, Lord Helsing need I remind you?" She took a calming breath. "Why didn't you tell me about your relationship with her? Why keep it a secret?"

He tried to pull her into his arms, but Charlotte pushed him away. "Don't touch me. Tell me why you didn't say anything?"

"Because I knew you'd react this way. Innocent or not, my actions with your cousin seem heartless. It was not my intention."

The thought of Mason with Rose turned Charlotte's stomach and made her tremble with jealousy. "Did you kiss her?"

He paused. "No."

The quiver in his voice gave him away. "You lie." Charlotte clasped her stomach and swallowed. Hard. "How could you lead her on so, then come to London and seek me out as you did. Kiss me, make love to me?"

"When I realized her attachment to me was beyond that of a friend, I left. I suppose I panicked. I know I should have stayed and let her down in the nicest way possible, but I didn't. Men kiss debutantes all the time, Charlotte, not all the mamas make them marry."

Charlotte scoffed. "You're a cad and I'm a whore. What am I doing?"

She pushed him away again when he went to pull her into his arms. "What we're doing is wrong and we need to stop. I'm married and you need a wife at some point." She sighed and met his troubled gaze. "Just the thought of you and Rose together made me insanely jealous. I can't stand it. But I can't help it, don't you see? You may not marry her, but you will marry someone, and what we're doing is only going to make it harder for me to let you go."

"Then don't let me go. I have a younger brother, Charlotte. He can produce the heirs for my family."

She shook her head. "If only it were that easy." Charlotte walked up to him and kissed his cheek, taking the opportunity to breathe in his delicious scent of sandalwood and something else, something exotic, one last time. "I know you want what's best for me, but my marriage mistake is the burden I must bear. Please leave me alone and go on with your life. I really do wish you well."

He stepped away from her and immediately she felt the loss of his heat. A lifetime loomed ahead of her, cold and bereft of any love, children, and solace.

"I will do as you wish but only because you've asked this of me. But let this be known, Charlotte. I neither agree nor want to. This decision of yours is yet another mistake made by you."

She gasped. "How can you say that to me?"

"Because it is true." He strode back to the door and paused before opening it. "I love you," he said, before taking his leave.

Charlotte slumped against the balustrade and tried to push down the severing pain tearing through her chest. "I love you too," she whispered, to nothing but the warm night air.

. . .

Mason stormed through the guests at the masquerade and didn't bother hiding his thunderous gaze. He entered the card room and found George sitting alone while he watched others around him play cards. Mason slumped into a vacant chair and summoned a footman for a brandy.

"Problem?" George drawled, smirking.

Mason cursed. "One of my own making. Damn it." He took the glass offered to him and drank it down without pause. "Charlotte's… I think I've ruined everything."

"Really? What did you do?"

"Why is it," Mason said, summoning the footman for another drink, "that women jump to conclusions that are inaccurate and then, will refuse to hear what you have to say."

George laughed. "You're asking the wrong man. I have no idea."

Mason took a calming breath and sat back in his chair. The brandy helped to cool his ire but Charlotte's words stung. That he'd fallen in love with her didn't help. With any other lady he'd have walked away without a backward glance at such an accusation from a married woman. But with Charlotte he couldn't. He cared for her. Her opinion mattered to him. That she thought him a cad who used debutantes and moved on to married women at will hurt. He shook his head.

"Miss Lancer's in town," Mason said not looking at George. The last thing he needed to see was his best friend's knowing smile.

"I see."

"I'm not sure of Miss Lancer's exact words to Charlotte but I was accused of using Miss Lancer for my own amusement in Bath. She even asked me if I'd kissed the girl."

"Had you," George asked, taking a sip of his drink. "I always wondered."

Mason ground his teeth. "I wouldn't call it a kiss. We were at a ball and she was upset over something trivial. I strolled with her about the pump room before I kissed her hand on departing. The way Charlotte was speaking, anyone would have thought that I lifted Miss Lancer's skirts and taken her there and then."

George frowned. "You did seem to take to the girl more than any other in Bath. Even you knew her attachment to you was growing."

Mason ran a hand through his hair. "I know, damn it. And I should have been more circumspect in my interactions with her. I made a mistake."

"And one I doubt Lady Remmick would be willing to forgive. You need to apologize and speak to Miss Lancer. Tell her that you're sorry but your affections lay elsewhere. And then speak to Lady Remmick and grovel at her silk slippers until she's inclined to forgive you as well."

"When did you become so knowledgeable?" Mason said, meeting his friends gaze for the first time.

"It's not something I like people to know, unless the need arises from a close friend."

Mason laughed. "Thank you."

"Don't thank me yet. Your apology hasn't been forgiven," George said.

Mason cringed and wondered just how he was to win Charlotte back and gain her forgiveness for a sin he never actually committed.

CHAPTER 11

A week later, Charlotte sat a circular table at Lady Bates' garden party and tried to keep her attention on the conversation going on around her. Yet, no matter how much she tried, the fact that Lord Helsing was present and right at this moment deep in conversation with Rose at another table, made it impossible to do so.

"If you keep looking over at them, he'll know you're wondering what they're talking about."

Charlotte took a sip of tea and raised her brow at Amelia. "I am wondering what they're talking about." She sighed. "I know. There is no hope for me."

Amelia laughed. "Yes there is. But your fixation is creating a little attention. Although I do believe they think your staring is due to the fact Lord Helsing is only days away from proposing to the girl."

Charlotte clenched her jaw at the thought of Rose and Mason married. Not that she didn't wish the very best for her dearest cousin and his lordship was certainly that, but because her life would continue on as before. With bouts of serenity followed by episodes of fear.

She heard laugher and clinking glasses and spied James flirting with some elderly matrons of the ton. He could certainly charm the ladies when he wished too. Pity he couldn't control his anger as well.

"I wrote to my father yesterday about James."

Amelia clasped her hand and smiled. "I'm glad you did. What do you think he'll do?"

Charlotte shrugged. "I'm not sure he can do anything. James is the one who'll have to initiate a divorce by catching me with another man. He'll never do it even if he had found out about me and Lord Helsing."

"I'm so sorry, Charlotte. I wish I could help in some way."

She smiled. "You do help by listening when I need someone to talk to. Like now for instance," Charlotte paused. "I'm going to ask James to depart for our country estate. I know he'll probably say no but if he doesn't then I'm going to leave instead. I'll not let him hurt me anymore."

"Under the circumstances I think this is a wise decision for you." Amelia cleared her throat. "Rose is coming—"

Charlotte looked up and the breath in her lungs hitched at the sight of Mason standing beside her cousin. His masculinity all but oozed from his attire and his casual elegance made her ache in all the naughty places on her body. She shifted on her chair and refused to react to his knowing grin.

"Lady Remmick," he drawled, picking up her hand and kissing it lightly.

Charlotte felt her mouth open before she realized what she was doing and closed it again. "Lord Helsing," she managed to say without sounding breathless like she felt. "Are you enjoying the garden party?"

"I am. The temptations she has on offer this afternoon positively make my mouth water."

Charlotte heard Amelia giggle and heat suffused her face. "Yes the cakes are very nice." Mason smiled and she knew he was laughing at her. She narrowed her eyes.

"Is it alright if I go and speak to Jane Carter, Charlotte? She's just arrived."

Charlotte nodded to Rose but didn't take her eyes off Mason. "Of course." She started when Mason sat beside her. Again, she was tempted by his very essence and she cursed herself for being a woman without willpower.

"Please, take a seat." Sarcasm all but dripped from her tone.

Lord Helsing watched her, his gaze intense and a shiver ran down her spine. Charlotte absently heard Amelia excuse herself and before she could join her friend, she felt a finger slide against her knee.

Charlotte shut her eyes for a moment and reveled in the contact before she pushed his hand away. "Don't."

"When can I see you again?"

Tension coiled inside the pit of her stomach and she almost moaned at the thought of being with him just one more time. Of having his lips on hers. All over her, in fact.

"You are seeing me," she said, laughing to hide her unease.

Mason leaned toward her. "I want to hear your voice rasp against my ear as I make love to you," he said, his breath but a whisper against her cheek.

Charlotte turned her attention to the other guests and realized with dismay the ladies once sitting at her table were no longer there. Cursing and thanking them for the small tidbit of privacy she met Mason's burning gaze and shook her head. "No."

His finger ran along her arm and she shivered.

"Yes," he said. "There is a room two doors up from the conservatory. Meet me there in half an hour or so. Please, we need to talk."

Charlotte squeezed her legs together as the temptation to be with him made it hard to remain immune. Mason stood and left before strolling about the lawns, talking to other guests at the party.

She took note of where Rose was and smiled as she watched a young gentleman amicably talk to her, his hands gesturing wildly with some tale.

Should she join him? The temptation to do so was beyond anything she'd ever known before. And Mason knew it. He knew what to say and do to her to make her crave him; want him, as desperately as she sensed he wanted her. And what did he have to say?

Seductive fiend.

Charlotte stood and noted Lord Helsing watching her from across the lawn. She walked over to Amelia and let her know where she was going before heading toward the house. Excitement thrummed through her veins and a smile quirked her lips. Poor, Mason. After she'd finished with him today, he'd never try and seduce her before the ton. Never again.

Mason watched Charlotte casually stroll toward Lady Bates' grand London home and his body tightened painfully. The unconscious sway of her hips pounded his blood directly to his groin and all he wished to do was clasp her delicate body hard against his and have her in any way possible.

He took note of Lord Remmick's whereabouts and noted with distaste the gentleman's attempt at flattery and polite behavior. The bastard didn't know the meaning of either word and he doubted if he ever would.

Mason walked toward a footman and taking a glass of champagne started to stroll toward the house. He entered off the terrace and headed toward the conservatory. The house was quiet and inside one could barely hear the party taking place out on the lawns.

Walking past the conservatory the smell of exotic plants and fruits wafted across his senses before he entered the room further on that he sought. Charlotte lounged on a chaise longue, her elegance of ease sending a frisson of uncertainty to course through him.

"Lord Helsing." She smiled and his gut clenched.

"My lady," he replied, snipping the lock on the door behind him.

"I would like to get a few things clear before we go any further. What is about to happen between us does not change what I said to you a week past at Lord Wilson's ball. Our liaison must end and you must marry. Is that understood?"

Mason ground his teeth but nodded. "I understand that as long as you know I'll always care for you. I also wish to clear up your confusion about Miss Lancer. I never seduced or kissed her. I always acted with the most gentlemanly behavior around your cousin. Today I apologized not having realized that she'd read more into our association than I had intended. She has forgiven me."

"Really?" She smiled and his gut clenched. "You never kissed her?"

"No," he replied walking toward her. "It's not Miss Lancer I want."

Charlotte held up her hand and he stopped. "I'd like to try something that I saw in a book once. You must allow me my way or I won't forgive you either."

Mason grinned. "What do you wish to do to me, my lady?" All sorts of erotic thoughts began racing through his mind.

"Come and sit on the day bed."

Mason did as she bid and watched as Charlotte knelt before him. The breath in his lungs hitched when she slid her hand up his thigh, his body wholly focused on what she was doing.

"I've been fascinated ever since I overheard some women talking as to whether a man could be pleasured in such a way. I searched out some books of James' and it seems to be true." She unclasped his frontfalls and Mason shifted in his seat. He moaned when she ran a finger down his length. "It is true, my lady," he managed.

"I enjoy your tongue against me. Love how wantonly you make me feel when I'm against your mouth."

"I'm more than willing to show you again, my dear." And he would if she'd allow it. Nothing in this world would please him more than to make Charlotte happy. He stilled when she kissed the end of his cock, her sweet, tongue tasting the very essence of him.

"It's my turn to make you moan, my lord."

Mason clenched his jaw, lest he follow through on his urge to thrust between her sweet lips. Dear God, how was he to get through this exquisite torture she had concocted for him. A quick learner, she licked down his length then took him wholly into her mouth. Heat and the lightest suction made his balls ache. "Charlotte."

She threw him a wicked smile and then continued her ministrations. Mason shut his eyes and prayed he had the stamina to last longer than he thought possible at this point. Her innocent loving of his member, her sweet sighs and moans as she tasted and enjoyed her attention to him near unmanned him.

Tension coiled inside as she relentlessly took his full length. Her goal to make him come, unfortunately all too close. "Charlotte, come away. You'll make me—"

"I want you to." She glided her hand up and down his length and he swallowed. Hard. "In my mouth. I want to taste you."

Mason watched as she continued to love him. He wanted to run his hands into her hair, hold her against him and fuck her mouth, but he could not. Instead, he saved the fantasy for another time and alternatively grabbed the daybed for support.

Lights blazed behind his eyelids as he came. His balls ached and never had an orgasm flowed throughout his body sending shivers of pleasure that consumed him. Charlotte moaned and kissed his member, making sure to lick the last drops of his essence before she sat back. "Did I please, my lord?"

Mason pulled her up on his lap and took her lips in a searing kiss. He let her know through his embrace, what she made him feel. What he would continue to feel for her if only she would let him. "Just knowing you're in this world pleases me, Charlotte. Everything else is a boon."

She laughed, the sound more carefree than he'd ever heard before and his heart thumped loud in his chest. "I meant what I said the other night, Charlotte."

She met his gaze, her own visage becoming serious at his tone. "What was that?"

Mason pushed a lock of hair from her brow. "That I love you."

Charlotte nodded, her eyes overly bright. "I know."

## CHAPTER 12

Two days later, Charlotte sat in the library of her London home and waited for James to wake up. He lay, sprawled on the settee before the unlit hearth, his clothing askew and an empty flask of liquor lying uncorked on the floor.

She thought about throwing a vase of water on his head, before common sense halted her actions. The conversation she was about to have with her husband would be bad enough. She didn't have to make it any worse.

When the lunch gong sounded, James stirred. She absently watched him wake up, his shaking hands and sickly demeanor no way resembling the man she had married. "When you're able I wish to speak to you, my lord."

He started at her voice and looked over the settee's back. "What do you want?" James rubbed his jaw and yawned. "Your lover owes me five-hundred pounds. Make sure he pays up."

Charlotte stemmed her urge to throw the blotter on

James' desk at his head. Instead she remained calm, and waited for him to join her. He heaved himself up from the lounge only to sprawl into his desk chair a moment later. Nerves churned in her stomach over the coming conversation.

"I want you to leave," she said, her voice stronger than she felt. "I have informed my father of your treatment of me and my desire to separate from you. You will leave this house today, or I will."

James threw his head back and laughed. Charlotte glared. "I mean what I say James. I'll no longer allow myself to be treated with unkindness and violence."

"You stupid whore. I'm not going anywhere and neither are you." He stood and Charlotte lifted her chin, refusing to give way to her fear of him. James came around the desk and leaned casually against its side, watching her silently.

"But then, I suppose I could divorce you and have you publicly shunned and termed a adulterer. It would certainly make our acquaintances happy knowing I'd be rid of the common trash I so wrongly married."

"Common or not I saved your estate with my money. You're a liar and a fraud. You give off this persona as someone loving, kind and charismatic when it pleases you and yet you're capable of the cruelest touch and words that I've ever known."

James shrugged, seeming not to care of his downfalls. "A divorce would ruin your sister's chances of a good marriage."

"Louise is old enough to look after herself. And over the last few months I've come to realize that if the gentleman who wishes to marry her would cry off because of my indiscretions as you call them, then he is not for her. I want my sister to marry for love and nothing less." Charlotte sat back and felt, deep inside her soul, that what she stated was true. Louise would never wish for her to continue living this type of life. A life that was no life at all.

For all her father's wish for his children to marry high into the peerage, his children themselves were never inclined to aspire to those great heights. And Louise would probably marry a local boy from the sphere in which they circulated in Somerset and be happier with her choice than any town dandy with status and great connections.

"So honorable," he scoffed. "And when we're divorced will you run off to your lover, Lord Helsing? Beg his lordship to marry you and try and redeem some sliver of your reputation."

"I have no immediate plans other than to move on with my life," she said without censure. "Now I asked you before and I'll ask you again. Which one of us is leaving? You or me?"

"Neither. Now get out. The sound of your voice droning on makes my head hurt."

Charlotte stood. "Good bye, James."

He clasped her arm, his grip painful, biting into her skin like tiny daggers. "Do not attempt anything foolish, Charlotte or you'll pay dearly for it."

"I've already paid dearly for my foolish action by marrying you. I've paid for it every, single day for the last two years." Charlotte wrenched her arm free and walked out the room. She chastised herself for the fear she felt whenever she was around him. It was like walking on cracked ice.

She heard James bellow for the carriage as she headed toward her bedroom. Charlotte rang for her maid and started to place the items she wished to take with her on her bed. Having received word from her father that he'd support her whatever decision she made, she began to prepare her departure to Grillon's Hotel.

Charlotte ignored her maid's shocked countenance when she told her of her plans, and instead thought over what she would do with her life away from James. Of course, if he chose to divorce her, she'd be ruined, but so would he be. She'd not allow him to come out of the trial in the House of Lords smelling of roses. No, Charlotte would ensure all his misdemeanors behind closed doors were aired along with any he could name against her.

When James sobered up and thought on his threat of divorce, he'd soon change his mind. No matter how much he hated her, or regretted their marriage, he wouldn't want anyone to know what type of man he was. It would seem she would have a separation but no divorce. Which would suffice, she mused, taking a watercolor painting down from the wall and placing it in a trunk. As long as she didn't have to live under the same roof as her abusive husband, her life would be much brighter. She was sure of it.

※

Later that day, Charlotte checked in at Grillon's and followed a footman to the second floor and her suite of rooms. The hotel in Albemarle Street had everything she'd hoped for, a drawing room for guests, a private bathing suite and a more than generous bedroom. Her maid had a small room adjoining the drawing room to enable her privacy.

Charlotte wrote a quick missive to Amelia, notifying her of her change of circumstances and contemplated informing Lord Helsing. She should probably let him know, and yet, somehow it seemed wrong to run to him as soon as she'd left her spouse. It was silly of her to think that way, but then, Mason couldn't marry her, so she should hold true to her wish for him marrying someone else. There were many women in London who'd suit him and could create a loving home he so deserved. And with her out of his life, he'd be free to pursue such a future.

Giving the missive to her maid to take downstairs, Charlotte looked about her new home and for the first time in an age, felt content. A feeling she could get used to, she was sure. Dinner arrived at seven and just as Charlotte was about to sit down at her small dining table, a knock sounded on her door.

Moments later, Amelia strolled into her suite, dressed in a high waisted green silk gown, her visage one of merriment. No doubt, Charlotte mused due, to her change in circumstance.

"I came as soon as I heard your news." Amelia joined her at table and nodded for some wine. "Lord Remmick would not leave, I gather?"

"He refused and threatened me not to do anything stupid." Charlotte paused. "It was time I stood up for myself and so I left."

"Does he know?"

A shiver raced down Charlotte's spine imagining how angry James would become when he found her gone. The poor staff would brunt most of his ire before he'd think to look for her. Not that she hoped he would. "Not yet," she said.

Amelia frowned and played with a diamond necklace about her neck. "You think he'll seek revenge in some way or make you return to him?"

Charlotte stood, no longer feeling hungry. "Of course he will. He'll probably demand I return home. But I won't, not under any circumstance. He can have my money and my reputation. I don't care anymore. Since being with

Lord Helsing, I've remembered what it is like to be alive again. How to love and be loved. I can never go back to James."

"You're in love with Lord Helsing."

It wasn't a question and Charlotte started at her friend's disclosure. "I am." And she was, more than anything in the world. Just the thought of Mason made her smile, her body heat and her heart sing. He was her everything and because he was so, she had to let him go. "But it doesn't matter as James will never divorce me and therefore my feelings for Mason are of no consequence. There is no future for us. He must marry and beget an heir. Something, that if you haven't noticed I've been unable to do for my husband.

"When it comes to Lord Remmick I cannot find fault for your inability to bear children, Charlotte." Amelia paused. "It is possible that the problem to have children lies with Lord Remmick and not you at all, dearest."

"Perhaps," Charlotte said, yet her two miscarriages which she'd told no one about made the problem seem all the more hers than anyone else. She pushed the distressing memory aside and sat on a chaise lounge. "I've told Lord Helsing he has to leave me alone and marry someone else. Thankfully, Rose has moved her attentions elsewhere, which I'm happy about."

"Where is Rose?" Amelia said, looking about the room.

"Aunt May arrived yesterday and they've gone to stay with her sister in law on Jermyn Street. I thought it only right to let my family know of my change of circumstance and Aunt May thought it best if Rose was distanced from me."

Amelia gasped and clasped her hand. "I'm so sorry, Charlotte. They do not understand what it would be like to live in such a distressing marital circumstance. I'm proud of you for leaving Lord Remmick. And as you know, Lord Furrow and I will always be ready to help you should you need anything."

Charlotte nodded and pulled her best friend into a hug. "I know and I thank you."

Amelia laughed. "You're very welcome."

## CHAPTER 13

It took a week for James to locate her. Charlotte stepped from Grillon's Hotel and breathed in the warm spring air before turning left and heading down Piccadilly. Her father had sent her some funds a few days ago and finally she was wholly independent from her husband.

The only blemish on her happiness was that Lord Helsing had not tried to seek her out either. And although Amelia had said he'd asked after her health at engagements she attended, Charlotte, did not understand why he never just asked outright where she was.

The memory of the lovemaking assailed her and along with it came excitement tinged with hurt. Did he not care or had he decided that her decree for him to marry another was right and had decided to act on it? What a silly fool she'd been. And yet...

"Charlotte!"

She stopped and looked across the street and spied James weaving his way through the local traffic. Anger all but thrummed along every line of his body and fear curdled in her stomach. Charlotte looked around, noted the many people about, and took some solace in the fact he wouldn't dare touch her on a public street.

Yet, his furious glare could prove her wrong.

"You will return to whatever hovel you're living, pack your things and return home immediately. How dare you make me a laughing matter for the ton of London?"

"Married couples live apart all the time. Our circumstances need not be any different." Charlotte lowered her voice. "And I will not return home, not under any circumstances."

"You bloody well will," he said, his tone laced with menace.

"I will not."

Out of nowhere, James hit her with his small walking cane. Charlotte put up her arm to fend off another strike when he raised his arm once more, yet the cane never came back down. She looked up and watched with awe as Mason broke the cane over her husband's back and threw him against a shop wall.

Never had Mason wanted to kill a man as much as he wished to kill Lord Remmick right at this moment. Having seen Charlotte on the street, he'd watched her stroll along the shop windows, her ease and happiness not something he'd seen glowing from her eyes since being back in London. But that had all changed the moment her brutal husband had seen her and taken her in hand. Literally.

He squeezed the filthy mongrel's throat and relished his fight for air. "If I ever see you come within an inch of Lady Remmick again I'll kill you. Do I make myself clear?" Mason released his windpipe a fraction so he could answer.

"She's my wife," Lord Remmick managed to gasp.

"Not anymore. From this day forward she isn't. Don't look for her and don't ever think that I don't know people who could make your disappearance seem like an accident," Mason said through clenched teeth. "Do I make myself clear?"

Lord Remmick tried to push him away and the urge to make the bastard pay assailed him. He stepped back a fraction then slammed his fist into his lordships gut before doing the same against his jaw. Charlotte's husband's head snapped back and hit the brick wall behind him before he slumped to the ground, unconscious."

Mason turned to Charlotte and pulled her back toward her hotel. "Are you all right?" he asked, trying to gauge her mood.

"I am, thank you." She stopped walking and Mason turned to her, wondering what she was thinking. She cast a quick look toward her husband and he noted her slight shiver. He wanted to pull her into his arms and show her that he'd never allow anything to happen to her. Neither by Lord Remmick's hand nor by anyone else's. If only she'd let him.

"Thank you Mason." Tears welling in her beautiful blue orbs. "You're my knight in shining armor."

"Always, Charlotte. Surely you know that by now," he said.

She nodded. "Did you mean what you said back there? That you'll protect me forever?"

"Yes. I know you think there is no future for us but you're wrong. As I said before, my brother is more than capable of keeping the family name and property in our rightful hands. I'm old enough to decide what I would like to do in my life. And that is to be with you. Come away with me. We'll move to the continent or New York. Start a new life where no one knows us."

She bit her lip and Mason felt like his heart would pump right out of his chest. Never had a reply mattered as much as Charlotte's did now.

"Yes. I'll go with you. Wherever you wish, just as long as we're together."

Mason smiled. "I love you Charlotte King."

Charlotte leant toward him and wrapped her arms about his neck. "I love you too," she said, kissing him.

Mason allowed the embrace to deepen and cared not a fig what anyone watching thought or said about their actions. From tonight, they would be on board the fastest ship to wherever they decided to go and London and its tonnish ideals – no one could ever live up to – could well and truly go to the devil.

# EPILOGUE

*Two Years Later – New York*

Charlotte threw the letter she'd received from her father, which had been accompanied by one from her late husband's solicitors and realized that she felt nothing but relief.

Mason walked into her parlor carrying their one month old daughter and a love so true filled her heart. True to his word, Mason had kept her safe and out of Lord Remmick's clutches and by doing so, they'd lived a life she'd never thought possible. Mason passed Lily to her and Charlotte kissed her beautiful little girl's pudding cheeks.

"What did the letter say," he asked, shuffling through the pages.

"Lord Remmick is dead. Was killed in some alley in East London. The solicitor wasn't very forthcoming in details but I'm sure you can imagine what happened."

Mason shook his head and came to sit beside her. "So I suppose we'll have to make you a lady again?"

Charlotte threw him a puzzled frown, wondering what he was talking about. "Excuse me?"

"Now that you're a widow, perhaps you'd prefer to be named a bride instead?"

Charlotte clasped his stubbled jaw and smiled. "Are you by any chance asking me to marry you, Lord Helsing?"

Mason took Lily onto his knee and turned their daughter to face Charlotte. "What do you think, Lily? Should Mama agree to marry Papa do you think?"

Charlotte laughed and kissed him quickly. "Of course I'll marry you. I love you."

"I love you more."

She shook her head, knowing such a thing could not be possible, but they could argue about that later. In bed. *Tonight.*

## LORDS OF LONDON SERIES
## AVAILABLE NOW!

Dive into these charming historical romances! In this six-book series by Tamara Gill, Darcy seduces a virginal duke, Cecilia's world collides with a roguish marquess, Katherine strikes a deal with an unlucky earl and Lizzy sets out to conquer a very wicked Viscount. These stories plus more adventures in the Lords of London series!

## FEED AN AUTHOR, LEAVE A REVIEW

If you enjoyed A GENTLEMAN'S PROMISE and would like to tell other readers your thoughts on the book, then please consider leaving a review at your preferred online bookstore or Goodreads.

## ALSO BY TAMARA GILL

Kiss the Wallflower series
A MIDSUMMER KISS
A KISS AT MISTLETOE
A KISS IN SPRING
TO FALL FOR A KISS
KISS THE WALLFLOWER - BOOKS 1-3 BUNDLE

League of Unweddable Gentlemen Series
FROM FRANCE, WITH LOVE
HELLION AT HEART
DARE TO BE SCANDALOUS
TO BE WICKED WITH YOU
KISS ME DUKE

Lords of London Series
TO BEDEVIL A DUKE
TO MADDEN A MARQUESS
TO TEMPT AN EARL
TO VEX A VISCOUNT
TO DARE A DUCHESS
TO MARRY A MARCHIONESS
LORDS OF LONDON - BOOKS 1-3 BUNDLE
LORDS OF LONDON - BOOKS 4-6 BUNDLE

To Marry a Rogue Series

ONLY AN EARL WILL DO
ONLY A DUKE WILL DO
ONLY A VISCOUNT WILL DO

A Time Traveler's Highland Love Series
TO CONQUER A SCOT
TO SAVE A SAVAGE SCOT

Time Travel Romance
DEFIANT SURRENDER
A STOLEN SEASON

Scandalous London Series
A GENTLEMAN'S PROMISE
A CAPTAIN'S ORDER
A MARRIAGE MADE IN MAYFAIR
SCANDALOUS LONDON - BOOKS 1-3 BUNDLE

High Seas & High Stakes Series
HIS LADY SMUGGLER
HER GENTLEMAN PIRATE
HIGH SEAS & HIGH STAKES - BOOKS 1-2 BUNDLE

Daughters Of The Gods Series
BANISHED-GUARDIAN-FALLEN
DAUGHTERS OF THE GODS - BOOKS 1-3 BUNDLE

## ABOUT THE AUTHOR

Tamara is an Australian author who grew up in an old mining town in country South Australia, where her love of history was founded. So much so, she made her darling husband travel to the UK for their honeymoon, where she dragged him from one historical monument and castle to another.

A mother of three, her two little gentlemen in the making, a future lady (she hopes) and a part-time job keep her busy in the real world, but whenever she gets a moment's peace she loves to write romance novels in an array of genres, including regency, medieval and time travel.

www.tamaragill.com
tamaragillauthor@gmail.com

Printed in Great Britain
by Amazon